HER BEAST

Beauty and the Captor Book 1

NICOLE CASEY

Copyright © 2017 by Nicole Casey. All Rights Reserved.

Without limiting the rights under copyright reserved above, no part of this publication may be reproduced, stored, or introduced into a retrieval system, or transmitted in any form, or by any means (electronically, mechanical, photocopying, recording or otherwise) without the proper written permission of the copyright owner, except in the case of brief quotations embodied in critical articles and reviews.

This book is a work of fiction. People, places, events and situations are the product of the author's imagination. Any resemblance to actual persons, living or dead, or historical events, is purely coincidental.

For those who like it *dark*.

— NICOLE

CONTENTS

Prologue	1
1. Scarlett	9
2. Scarlett	25
3. Derek	49
4. Scarlett	63
5. Derek	99
6. Scarlett	125
7. Derek	151
8. Scarlett	177
Acknowledgments	203
More Information	205

PROLOGUE

Derek

I'd done a good job. I acknowledged to myself as Senor Ruiz came to retrieve his latest acquisition. But I wasn't proud. Marcos was proud; it was clear by the way his eyes glowed with approval. He patted me on the back as the other man took hold of the lead and led the product of weeks of mind-bending work out of the room. My work. Countless hours of work.

"This one was important, and I knew you wouldn't let me down, son," Marcos congratulated me as he motioned for a servant from across the room. "You never fail to impress me."

The servant appeared at his side seconds later, holding open a box of Cuban cigars. Marcos selected two from the box and handed me one before striking a match to light mine and then his own. I inhaled deeply, savoring the familiar taste of a victory cigar. The earthy, tobacco flavor slid across my tongue as the pungent smoke perfumed the air.

As I'd grown into the life that had been laid out for me, I'd come to view Marcos in some shady area between friend and father. I remembered waiting for moments like these, anxious for my hard work to amount to something in his eyes. Years later, there was none of that eagerness now, but a quiet hum of satisfaction nonetheless.

As Senor Ruiz made his way down the long hall, I couldn't help but watch the symbol of my success. Her hips swayed as she crawled gracefully down the hall, her head down and her body naked except for the leather collar around her slim neck. She hesitated for just a moment as she reached the door, and I felt the familiar tightening in my gut. She'd performed flawlessly for the past two weeks, and I hoped she wasn't reverting to old habits. But with a swift tug on the leash attached to her collar, she crawled out the door, and I lost sight of her.

Yes, I'd done a good job. The girl had been stubborn and prideful the day she'd been brought to me, but not anymore. Now, she would make an ideal slave for her new master. I breathed a sigh of relief. It wasn't only the embarrassment of her slipping up that had worried me, but rather, after so long working with this one, I'd long since tired of her. I was ready for a new challenge, something that would send more than an innate sizzle of arousal through my veins.

It wouldn't last long. It never did. One slave was no different from the next, even in the early days before they were conditioned for sale. They fought and they pleaded, but quickly they gave up the fight, allowing me to mold them into precisely what they needed to be.

"You were built to command, my son," Marcos said, drawing my attention back.

I wasn't built for this, some part of me wanted to shout. But the truth of the matter was…I was. I'd watched the other men working with the slaves for years, and not even the most experienced of them had acquired complete domination over a spineless, young girl in the time it had taken me to turn the obstinate daughter of Marcos' biggest rival into an adept slave.

"And in celebration of your success, I have a surprise for you," he continued, draping his arm around my shoulder and leading me down the hall to his office.

I didn't like surprises. Surprises meant unexpected, and I liked to know what to expect. Still, I confess I was mildly curious. Marcos' body seemed to be thrumming with anticipation.

Once inside his office, he placed a file folder down on the desk and motioned for me to take it. Another job? Another slave? This wasn't my idea of a surprise, but I opened up the folder to see what was inside. And then I saw the photo lying on top of a neat stack of papers. My stomach clenched and my rusted heart thudded heavily in my chest. It was him—the man who had taken everything from me. James Donovan.

"Where is he, Marcos?" I was no longer tired. I was primed, ready. An old rage pulsed through my veins and my fingers shook with impatience. I could feel the cold steel of the Glock in my hand, hear the grind of steel against steel as I cocked it. I could even envision Donovan's face in that split second before the bullet tore through his body. I'd longed for this moment and I'd waited for so long.

"No, Derek."

"No? What do you mean no?" Why the hell was he dangling the man in front of me just to deprive me of the vengeance that was, by right, mine?

"I mean, I am not going to let you rush into this hastily. It will be over too quick, and you'll be left with nothing but the bitter taste of disappointment. Your revenge cannot be swift."

I wanted to argue with him. I'd wanted Donovan dead for so long, the idea of postponing the kill even a minute longer felt almost unbearable. But Marcos was right. I wanted him dead, yes, but I also wanted him to suffer. I'd regret acting on impulse, no matter how strong that impulse was.

I took a deep breath, hoping the smoke-tinged air would somehow infuse my body with even a modicum of the calm I'd felt just moments ago. "What did you have in mind, Marcos?"

"James Donovan's wife is dead, but he has a daughter. And you, Derek, have a very unique set of skills."

Hmm. Well, it wasn't the most original plan—since it was the exact same method of revenge Marcos had used on his own rival, but it was effective. Take the thing of most importance to a man and make him watch as you broke it and transformed it into a shell of what it once was.

I'd already known Donovan had a daughter. Even twelve years later, I could vaguely remember the feisty little redhead with eyes that were too big for her face and a chip on her shoulder. If there was any of that girl left in her now, she'd pose an even bigger challenge than the last slave. But there were few things in life better than a good challenge.

"You know where she is?" I asked though I was already certain he did.

Marcos nodded.

"I want to get a look at her, and then I'll send Vito and Alejandro to pick her up."

"I think you're making a wise decision, my friend," he said, patting me on the back once again.

A short flight, and an even shorter drive later, I sat in a nondescript Lexus across from a dilapidated looking park. The girl would be turning the corner onto the street any minute—like she did every day at precisely 8:45 in the morning on her way to work—according to Marcos' carefully gathered intel.

Fuck me, I breathed, as she turned onto the street. The hair was the same—a fiery auburn that put copper redheads to shame—but everything else about her had changed. She was tall, and though the shapeless coat and clothing she wore did nothing to accentuate it, it was obvious she was slim. She moved with a kind of grace I hadn't seen before, and the gentle sway of her hips beneath her bulky clothing had me following her every movement, like the hypnotizing swing of a pendulum.

As she came closer, I could see that her oval face had lost all traces of its childhood pudginess, and her eyes, though larger than the typical woman's, fit into the delicate features of her face perfectly. Something about the look in her eyes though told me she was lost, not geographically, but as if part of herself was missing. She looked in-need, though nothing about her made her appear needy.

I fought the sudden urge to get out of the car. I wanted to take her back with me now. I wanted to bend her. Shape her. Make her needy for nothing but the will of her master. But I stayed where I was. The plan had been set, and I wouldn't deviate from it in my haste to have this beauty.

She would come soon enough.

1

SCARLETT

I skimmed through the photos as they came out of the film-developing-machine. I was supposed to flip through them quickly and then shove them in an envelope for our customers, but I never did that. I liked the pictures because no one ever took snapshots of the sad moments in their life. It was always the happy memories caught on camera.

I look at the photos, and I imagine what life has in store for them next. It's silly, of course, but I've been told I'm a natural born storyteller. And so, I fill in the missing pieces between snapshots. Like what had happened after the

Robinson's returned from their honeymoon in Aruba—a trip that had used up nearly a dozen rolls of film? Did she quickly realize the man couldn't screw the cap back on the toothpaste to save his life? Did he wonder how the hell the woman could possibly need three dozen pairs of shoes? I imagine their first fight came quickly—because they're both passionate and stubborn people. In the end, though, they'll always work it out. They aren't perfect, and they'll spend a lot of time-fighting, but they love each other. And so long as they never forget that, they'll be OK.

And what about Lindsay Miller's graduation photos? I think she'll meet her first serious boyfriend in college. He'll be a great guy, but after a year or two, they'll realize they just aren't right for each other. But they won't part on angry terms, and they'll even get together for coffee a couple of times after a nasty breakup or particularly bad exam. Five years later when she's finished college and found Mr. Right, she'll even invite her first love to her wedding, and just for a minute, both of them will wonder if they'd made a mistake breaking up.

Hey, it's not picture-perfect all the time—I said I was a good storyteller, not a fabricator of fairy tales.

Why did I do it? It all came down to the same thing, really: to create a life that existed beyond this moment, because if it existed for them, it could exist for me, too, right?

The bell above the door to the shop jingled, and I shoved the stack of photos in my hand into the waiting envelope as nonchalantly as I could. It was all well and good to daydream about customers' lives; it was another thing entirely to get caught doing it. Aside from looking like a nosy snoop, I was fairly certain there were laws against this sort of thing—or at least company policies that discouraged peeping-tom employees.

Fortunately, the customer who had just walked in and caught me unaware was Mrs. Jenkins, and while the woman had a heart of gold, she had the eyesight of a potato. I'd developed her film a half hour ago, and it was obvious she had taken the pictures herself since half the prints were of the inside of the lens cap.

It was rather strange for the woman to be out so late, but the reason became clear a moment later when her son walked in with a half-crazed gleam in his eyes. His hands were full of bags from every store on the strip—they'd been Christmas shopping. She couldn't get around on her own, and her son stepped up to help her out as often as he could. There were limits to just how many tea cozies, handmade quilts and lace doilies a person could peruse before they went a little screwy. And it looked like Mr. Jenkins Jr. had passed that mark about an hour ago.

"Good evening, Mrs. Jenkins, Mr. Jenkins. Enjoying the weather?"—the usual small talk through which two or more people completely ignored what they would really like to say in favor of the same pleasant, but meaningless banter ad nauseam. I was very good at small talk. I'd spent most of my life engaged in nothing but small talk. My father wasn't the meaningful conversation-type.

"It's lovely, dear," she replied while her son nodded and ran his fingers through the sparse hair on the top of his head, making it stick straight up. I didn't think he cared. Since he looked about two minutes away from ripping it out from the roots, what difference did it make if it stood on end?

Something else registered in his eyes a moment later though, as his gaze darted back and forth between the envelope of photos in my hand and my chest. I turned away and took as much time as I could retrieving and opening a bag for Mrs. Jenkins photos. I didn't want him to look at me that way. I didn't want any of them to look at me that way.

I slipped the envelope into the bag and turned around to hand it to Mrs. Jenkins while I kept my eyes carefully averted from her son. A few more mundane pleasantries and the pair bustled out the door, hoping to squeeze in a little more shopping before the stores closed up for the night. I checked the clock—five more minutes and I was done for the day, too. And since it was unlikely anyone would come dashing in at the last minute, I shut down the developer machine and started to close out the cash register.

Six minutes later, I closed and locked the door

behind me. The busy street was still filled with people making away with their last-minute purchases. I watched them for a moment. What had they been shopping for? Christmas presents for parents and children, nieces and nephews? Who were they in a hurry to get home to?

A young woman darted across the street to her car, bags flapping at her side. I imagined she'd just found the perfect present for her impossible mother-in-law. She was hurrying home to show off her find to her husband, and he'd pretend to be vexed that she'd found the better present. Really though, he was happy that his wife put so much effort into the woman who could be more than difficult to get along with sometimes.

OK, that was a little fairy-tale-ish, but it was Christmastime. I was allowed to be a bit fanciful. Reality could kiss my ass.

The woman dropped her bags in her trunk and slipped into the car, and as if that was my cue, I turned away and started down the street in the opposite direction. I stayed on the main street for a block and a half, but then veered off through the parking lot of the Cash n' Carry—it took four minutes off the walk home. During the warm, summer months I didn't mind the extra time to get home, but it was winter now, and the wind had picked up. It billowed up my calf-length skirt and snuck up the sleeves of my long, puffy coat. I could even feel it testing the edges of my knitted hat as it tried to find a way in. I pulled my hat down further, so low that my eyelashes brushed against the brim when I blinked.

Three more blocks and I'd be home, though that prospect was always met with conflicting emotions. The temperature was warm there, but the company was ice cold. It was home though. Right now, with the chilly evening air biting my skin, I'd be content to hide away in my room all night if it meant escaping the bitter wind's persistent assault. I picked up my pace, ignoring the way my cold muscles objected. And the speed helped. It warmed the core of my body and spread some of that heat to my shoulders and thighs.

Suddenly, a loud screech sounded behind me. It made me skitter forward several steps. It was so close I thought whatever made the sound was going to plow right into me.

I spun around to find the front bumper of a van less than a foot from my calves. The wind had been blowing so hard I hadn't heard it approach. Nothing but that piercing screech. The driver must have lost control of the vehicle on a patch of ice, and I breathed a grateful sigh, realizing that a few more inches and it could have splattered me like a bug on a windshield. Yes, maybe that was a bit melodramatic, but could you blame me after such a close call?

The driver got out of the vehicle, and I waved to him, letting him know I was fine. While I appreciated his concern, it was still just as cold out now as it had been thirty seconds ago. Since there was no harm done, I didn't want to hang around to see if I could get frostbite.

"I'm fine, really," I called above the wind when he continued to approach.

The passenger door opened at the same time, and another man stepped out. He looked unassuming; tall, but lanky. He was probably just concerned I'd been hurt.

Their approach was casual enough that I couldn't pinpoint any particular reason to be frightened, but an icy shiver tremored down my spine that had nothing to do with the cold wind whipping my long braid against my face.

I hadn't had a whole lot of run-ins with creepy freaks, but I wasn't about to stick around to find out if this was one such occasion. So, I turned on my heels and took off like a sprinter. I'd wanted to try out for the track and field team in my last year of high school, but my father had never let me. Right then though, I bet I put the school's best runner—Julie Wells—to shame. The ground was a blur beneath my feet and the trees that lined the street whipped by.

I heard footsteps behind me, heavy and fast. They were following me, running after me. But I was fast. I could beat Julie Wells around the school's track course with both hands tied behind my back. So, I fought against the panic that welled in my chest and willed my legs to go faster.

Faster.

But their footsteps grew louder. And louder.

Oh god, they were close.

Within seconds, they were right behind me. Their heavy footfalls sounded against the pavement in cadence with my own. I tried to speed up, to stretch my legs out farther, but I was losing ground fast.

A hand gripped my arm from behind, and I screamed, silently cursing Julie Wells for making me think I was fast. The hand yanked me back so hard my feet came out from under me.

I kicked and flailed, but the vice-like grip on my arm didn't relent. I felt like a marionette hanging awkwardly on one string.

I screamed louder as panic filled my chest. My breath came faster and my heart beat wildly. I could feel my pulse pounding in my head. I wasn't beat yet though. I couldn't give in, I had to fight.

I struggled to get my feet beneath me, and the moment I did, I lunged upward, not to my full height, just high enough to sink my teeth into the meaty hand on my arm. I bit hard, thanking the stars for the incisor teeth

I'd always thought were just a little too sharp.

They were the only weapon I had, and I sunk them deep into the hand. A thick, metallic-tasting liquid flooded my mouth. I'd done damage—I knew it, but still, the bleeding hand held firm. Out of the corner of my eye, I saw another hand coming at me—fast.

And the next thing I knew I was lying on the ground. At first, a surge of victory flooded my veins. I'd won. I was free.

My shoulder hurt and my head throbbed, but I'd done it—I'd made him release me. I felt feral...powerful...

...And then I felt like a caged animal. A hand gripped each of my arms and yanked me upright. The faces that hadn't seemed threatening when the man had stepped out of the van just a moment ago now twisted into evil sneers.

"You're going to pay for that, bitch!" the man with the bloody hand growled while the two of them dragged me back toward their vehicle.

I dug my feet into the ground, but it did little to slow their pace.

I screamed.

They continued unperturbed.

And I knew why. A block ago, someone would have heard me. Someone would have rushed out to help, or called the police...or done something. But here, there was a rundown park to one side of me and an abandoned apartment building on the other. My only hope was that someone would be passing by like I had been. Still, it was hope, and I latched on, screaming so loud it hurt my own ears, and whipping my head back and forth, searching for someone—anyone. Please, anyone!

There was no one.

Beside the van, Bloody-hand started to open the door, but he jerked his hand away. I must have bitten into something substantial. He howled in pain.

It gave me a brief moment's satisfaction to know I'd done some serious damage, and it renewed my dwindling hope of escape. I'd hurt him once; I could do it again.

But my hope was short-lived. Both hands

shoved me, and I fell forward, banging my forehead against the carpeted floor of the van.

"Dose her," Bloody-hand snarled.

That didn't sound good—rather ironic, though. I'd spent my entire teenagehood avoiding every street drug and stolen prescription drug that circulated my high school, and these two buffoons were going to drug me? It probably shouldn't have been the first thought to occur to me, but it was almost surreal. Two minutes ago, I'd been hurrying home like any other normal day. And now...now I was desperately clinging to the fleeting hope I could escape these monsters.

In two minutes, I'd gone from normal to fighting for my life. And I was losing.

A weight pressed against my back—an elbow, maybe—and it stopped me from throwing my body backward, but I couldn't stop fighting. I raised my feet off the ground and kicked out, again and again. My boots weren't pretty—I didn't wear pretty things—but they were sturdy. If I could just make contact, I knew it would buy me a second or two.

Something sharp jabbed my neck. It took me a second to realize what it was—a needle. When they'd said they were going to dose me, I envisioned one of them plugging my nose while the other forced me to swallow a bunch of pills. I hadn't anticipated this. How could I have? My life had been normal two minutes ago.

I tried to kick out again, but my foot flopped limply back to the ground.

Again.

This time, I could barely make my leg move at all. My legs were so heavy. My whole body felt heavy actually, though I don't know how that was possible since the rest of me was lying on the scratchy carpet. Could something seem heavy if you weren't trying to lift it?

When my eyelids grew heavy, the panic I'd been holding at bay flooded my chest. I couldn't keep it back any longer. Whatever they'd injected me with was doing this, and in a few seconds, I was going to be unconscious—I just knew it—and there wouldn't be a damn thing I could do to stop them.

I screamed in my head, too weak to open my

mouth to let the sound out. And then I was even too weak to do that, and I drifted into oblivion.

It was only in that last moment of consciousness the thought hit me; would I ever wake up again?

2

SCARLETT

I came awake slowly, but right away I knew it wasn't the first time I'd woken up since slipping into a drug-induced unconsciousness in the back of their van. The last time was cloudy, but it was there. I remembered bits and pieces. I was on a bed, and I was struggling with them. Their hands had been everywhere, ripping and tearing at my clothes. Brutal grips as I was turned this way and that, pinched and squeezed.

I recalled pleading, but it had done nothing. And then, when they'd torn off my bra, I'd gone berserk, kicking and flailing and screaming.

And then nothing.

Had they jabbed me with another needle? Or knocked me unconscious? By the way my head was throbbing from a focal point in the back, I figured I could guess which one.

But then what? What had they done when I was no longer fighting them, no longer even conscious to make the weakest of protests?

Fear lodged in my throat when I thought about the most likely thing they'd done. They'd been stripping me—on a bed. What else could their intentions have been?

But mentally assessing myself, I didn't feel any different. There was no soreness between my thighs to suggest they'd used me that way. I could feel everything else—my shoulder ached, my arms hurt where they'd first grabbed me. And I could feel every bump and bruise from their rough-handling of me. But not that. They hadn't raped me.

But why not? Were they waiting until I was conscious again? Is that what they wanted?—for me to fight them, knowing I was going to lose? If I continued to lay here, eyes closed and perfectly still, would they get bored with me, or think they'd done some sort of irreversible damage with their last blow?—no fun to play with a brain-damaged victim, was it? It was my best plan at the moment, or rather, my only plan until I could come up with something better.

So, I did my best to keep my breathing steady and keep my eyes closed without squeezing them too tightly-shut and giving myself away. I tried to keep my limbs still, but that was lowest on the priority list. It seemed reasonable that the body might move innately when unconscious like it did in ordinary sleep.

And then I moved on to assessing my situation.

I was on a bed, presumably the same one I'd woken up on before, but that was little help because I hadn't had the time to look around and survey my surroundings then.

I was naked—I cringed mentally at the realization, but I struggled to keep my features smooth. But I could feel the same comfortably warm air across every inch of my body that wasn't pressed against the mattress. My legs had been left—or positioned—slightly parted, and I felt an overwhelming urge to squeeze them shut. I resisted—just barely.

There was no noise in the room aside from my relatively stable breathing, which suggested there was no one else here. That made it tempting to open my eyes, but not yet. For all I knew, it was a really big room and I just couldn't hear the others breathing.

All right, so, I was naked, on a bed, in a room, the door to which may or may not be locked, and the men who'd done this to me may or may not be in the room with me. So far, this wasn't looking very good for me.

I ever so slowly moved one hand from where it laid near my side, just enough to ascertain the likelihood of whether I'd been restrained. My hand seemed to move freely though, which made it unlikely.

That was at least one relief. If they did come at me again, I'd have some small chance of catching them off-guard and escaping—through the door which may or may not be locked. Still, that sounded like the beginnings of a plan to me. Not a good one, but better than nothing.

I'd listen for the sound of them approaching and the moment they did, I'd spring away and out the door—assuming it wasn't locked from the outside or with a key. There was no point in worrying about it—there was no way for me to know ahead of time. And there was no sense in trying to fight them. I'd failed miserably on more than one attempt, and feared it would inevitably only lead to a repeat.

But minutes ticked by and still no movement. Maybe they'd just left me here for good. But just as I was beginning to entertain the possibility, I heard the grind of a lock and a door opened a second later.

I did my damnedest to fight the panic rising in my chest. I wanted to scream, to run, not to lay here and wait patiently for them to approach. But by some miracle, I was able to do it.

As the intruders came closer though, I realized there was only one set of footsteps. Not two. Where was the other one? Was he waiting by the door?—blocking it to impede my escape? Damn it. With my eyes closed and no sounds other than the single set of footsteps, I had no way of knowing. And I didn't exactly have a whole lot of time to modify the plan. So, I'd stick with the original, and if there was an obstacle in my way, I'd find some way to charge right through it. Maybe there was something I could grab quickly to use as a weapon—like a lamp, or even a heavy book—and I could throw it or ram it into him.

The footsteps were only a couple of feet away, and I could hear him breathing. The sound was faint but somehow reassuring. He wasn't some kind of larger-than-life monster. He was just human. Flesh and blood. And I could do this.

He stopped right next to the bed, but be remained there. I'd swear I could feel his eyes on me and the urge to cover up skyrocketed. Not yet. Don't do it, I cautioned myself. I wondered which one it was. The one I'd bit or the one who'd jabbed me with the needle? It didn't really smell like either of them. In fact, it smelled nothing like them. It was a heady, woody scent, with an undertone of something that could only be described as one hundred percent male—not the old sweat and gym socks kind of 'male', but virile, the kind of scent a woman couldn't help but notice—apparently, no matter the situation.

"I know you're awake," a voice spoke from next to the bed—a voice I'd never heard before. It was clear and deep, with the faintest hint of an accent—though I couldn't place what kind. It definitely wasn't either of the men I'd been expecting.

I resisted the urge to open my eyes. Yes, I'd probably been busted, and it seemed like there was little point in keeping up the charade. But it was possible it was a trick, that he was just trying to find out if I was awake.

So caught up in thought, I wasn't prepared for it when a finger brushed across my lips. I hadn't been expecting it. His touch was gentle and fleeting, not like the way the other men had mauled at me.

My eyes flew open and I gasped. This was certainly not what I'd been expecting, though it rather lined up with the scent of him. The man was beautiful. Well, maybe that was a poor choice of words since there wasn't anything feminine about him. But handsome was just too weak a word to describe the man hovering above me. Dark hair, vivid blue eyes, perfectly balanced features, a strong jaw...the list went on, but the eyes kept drawing me back. For the briefest of moments, they even put me at ease, as if I knew somehow they were a comfort, not a danger.

But then logic won out and I scurried off the bed, away from him, dragging the covers from the bed with me as I went. There was no one standing in the doorway to block my exit, but the door was closed. I hadn't heard him close it, and I could only hope he hadn't had the sense to lock it.

I dashed to the door, but the handle wouldn't budge. I kept trying it anyway, expecting to feel his hands latch on me from behind at any moment, but they didn't.

Abandoning the door, I spun around to fight him off, but he was still standing next to the bed, though he wore an amused expression now and his vivid eyes were filled with heat.

I spotted another door out the corner of my eye, and I ran for it, hoping it might lead me to an escape before the cocky man came after me. But it was a bathroom, I realized once I'd made it through the door uninhibited. An enormous walk-in shower and giant bathtub...but, not a single door or window.

It made sense now why he hadn't bothered wasting his energy coming after me—there was nowhere for me to go. I stayed in the bathroom with the bedcover wrapped around me, huddled in one corner as if I could will the wall to swallow me up.

It didn't.

His footsteps sounded quietly across the carpet, and I pressed my body harder against the wall. He stopped at the doorway, wearing the same amused grin. If I wasn't terrified, I would have wanted to slap that cocky expression right off his too-handsome face. As it was though, I had no intentions of coming out of my corner —maybe ever.

After a moment he turned away and walked over to the bathroom sink. I wished I'd picked a corner in the other room because even though the bathroom was bigger than any I'd seen, it was still too small. His presence seemed to take up too much of the precious space between us.

He picked up a plastic cup sitting next to the facet, turned on the sink and filled it up. A strange time to stop for a drink, wasn't it?

But when he turned off the facet, he started toward me and I pressed back so hard against the wall that it felt like the tile on the wall behind me was digging into my bones.

He stopped maybe two feet away and extended the hand holding the cup. He was giving me water? Why? And then he extended his other hand and opened it up. There was a pill in it—ibuprofen, I recognized. Again, why?

"I imagine you must have quite the headache," he said and extended both hands a little further.

Confused, but recognizing the truth in what he said, I clenched the blanket tighter against me with one hand and took the proffered pill with the other. I popped it into my mouth and reached for the glass, sipping just enough to swallow the pill. Since he'd brought it up, I'd become much more aware of the pain throbbing at the back of my head, and was hopeful the pill would provide some relief. It was difficult to think clearly the way it was pounding. Every beat reverberated through my head.

I handed the glass back and doubled up my grip on the blanket. He took the cup and placed it back on the sink and then returned to where he'd been standing in front of me. He didn't make any move to touch me. He just stood there. The silence stretched out, winding its way through our frozen tableau and making me feel even jumpier than I'd been.

What the hell did he want from me? Was this a game?—some twisted way of drawing out the anticipation of what was coming? Or was he their lackey?—sent to keep an eye on me until they came back? No, I dismissed the last thought. This man was nobody's lackey. His clothes, his posture, the tilt of his chin, the aura that radiated from him, the cocky smile, the steely control in his eyes—this man did nobody's bidding but his own.

So, what did that make him?—the ringleader? He was the alpha who demanded the first bite, and when he was finished the others could have whatever scraps he left behind?

"What...what do you want?" I stuttered in a weak and pathetic voice.

"Ah, you can speak. I was beginning to doubt what Alejandro and Vito had to say about your wicked tongue."

My wicked tongue? They'd kidnapped me, stripped me and knocked me unconscious, and I was the one with the 'wicked' anything?

"Why don't we have a seat and talk?" he suggested, motioning back toward the other room.

I didn't want to sit or talk, but at least getting out of this room would put some distance between us. So, I nodded, and then waited for him to leave the room first.

I breathed a small sigh of relief when he'd stepped through the doorway, taking with him the feeling of claustrophobia that had begun to creep in on me, and then I followed him out slowly. But when he sat down on the edge of the bed, I stopped where I was. I was not going to sit on the bed with this man, and since there were no other seats in the room, I decided I was fine right where I was.

"Come closer," he said in a tone that made it seem like keeping my distance was silly, and yet, two more steps and that was as close as I was going to get.

He chuckled and seemed to let it go. "The first

rule you will learn is you will obey. If you don't, you will be punished however I see fit. Do you understand?"

Understand? No, I certainly did not understand. What the hell was he talking about?

"No," I cried and backed up several steps.

"No, you don't understand? Or no, you won't obey?" he asked easily.

He had to be crazy. "No, I don't understand what the hell you're talking about, and no, I will not obey you. You don't own me."

"You may not understand, Pet, but you will come to obey me, I assure you."

I stood there frozen, my mind reeling in shock. This couldn't be happening. It was beyond insane.

"Now, remove the blanket."

What? No! Hell, no. I clutched the blanket tighter against me and glared back at him.

"I won't tell you again," he said, and though I could tell he meant it, and I didn't even want to guess at what he was going to do, I stood there stiffly, refusing to relinquish it.

He sighed heavily and rose to his feet. He moved gracefully, like a lion, and I had a sinking feeling I was his prey. He kept coming until he was right in front of me and his presence was ten times more overwhelming—and scary—than it had been in the bathroom. He didn't look angry. His breathing hadn't changed and his hands were unclenched, relaxed at his sides, but I knew looks could be deceiving.

I should have run, retreated back to my corner in the bathroom, but he would just follow me there, so I stood my ground.

"I'll make this easy for you, Pet. Kneel." His voice was little more than a whisper, but he didn't need to talk louder. His lips were just inches from my ear.

He wanted me to kneel?—like a dog? I wasn't some animal he could tame. "I'm not a dog," I snapped at him.

"No, you most certainly are not," he agreed as he ran a finger down my jaw. "But you will kneel and you will give me that blanket."

"Never," I barked.

"We'll see about that," he said, and in a flash, he had my wrists trapped in one, big hand and he was dragging me toward the bed.

I dug in my heels, but I was no match for his strength, and he pulled me with him easily. Once there, he untucked a pair of shackles that had been concealed between the mattress and the box spring and hooked them on my wrists.

I tugged, but the shackles were attached to somewhere in the bed. I was trapped, hunched over at the side of the bed. I couldn't even stand upright. The blanket had bunched around my waist as he'd dragged me, and he yanked it off, leaving me completely exposed, with no way of covering myself.

I cried and screamed and tugged against the restraints, but it was no use.

"You may kneel, and I will punish you for your disobedience with my hand. Or you can refuse, and I will use my belt."

That's why he'd trapped me like this, with more than enough slack to go down on my knees, but not enough to stand up, keeping me in a perfect position to…to punish me.

I screamed louder, hurting my own ears and making my headache more. I twisted and turned in a futile effort to get away while he stood there beside me, just out of reach so I couldn't even lash out at him. I saw his hands move to his waist, unbuckling the strap of leather…

"Please let me go," I pleaded in the same futile effort. He wasn't going to let me go—maybe ever.

He shook his head and then moved behind me, and I knew I had about three seconds left to make a choice. I couldn't stop this from happening, and the belt was going to hurt a lot more than his hand. But still, I couldn't force my legs to comply. They would not obey, no matter the consequences. Maybe it was still too unreal. Perhaps I couldn't believe he would actually do it, that he could actually spank a complete stranger with his belt.

But then I felt his hands on me, grazing over my backside. My attention had been diverted to escape, first from the room and then from his belt, but now I became painfully aware of my state of undress. I was completely naked, bent over more than enough for him to see every part of me. No one had seen me there, and I didn't want him there now, looking at me, touching me.

Without warning, his hand left my flesh and I felt the sting of his belt, like a lash of fire across my cheeks. I cried out, gripping the bottom of the mattress when my knees threatened to buckle.

Another lash of fire crisscrossed the first. I screamed so loud my throat started to ache.

Another, and then another, and I couldn't stop my knees from giving out. I sobbed in between screams. He had what he wanted—I was kneeling before him now.

But the belt came down again, lower, across the backs of my thighs. "Stop! What the hell do you want from me?"

He had what he wanted. Why wouldn't he stop?

The belt struck me again, across my cheeks, on top of a previous strike and blazing ten times hotter.

"You did not obey, Pet. Your knees gave out on you," he said when he stopped, but then he spanked me again, and the fire made my whole body jerk against the bed. And then again.

"Are you ready to obey?"

"Yes," I sobbed pathetically as a steady stream of tears dripped down onto my naked breasts.

He dropped the belt on the bed and bent down to unshackle me. He didn't seem the least bit worried that I'd grab for his belt and give him a taste of his own medicine. But of course he wasn't worried—he was infinitely stronger than me. The sick freak could have easily pushed me down on my knees if he'd wanted to, but he'd wanted to hurt me and humiliate me. And if I lunged for that belt, I had no doubt he'd do it again.

"Now, turn around and face me. And kneel."

I hated him. He was sick and twisted and evil. And somehow I would make him pay for this. For now, though, I couldn't take one more lash across my flaming backside, so I scooted around on my knees and sat back, almost on my heels, when I faced him. Keeping my thigh muscles squeezed tight, I was able to keep myself elevated just enough to stop my heels from digging into the fresh welts that had no doubt risen across my skin.

"Very good, Pet. Next time, don't make it so difficult for yourself. It will be much easier for you here if you understand that obedience is mandatory."

I kept my mouth shut. I wanted to tell him where he could shove his obedience, but I wasn't stupid enough to do it. Or maybe I just wasn't brave enough. I'd never had to be brave, not like this. And I wasn't feeling it in overwhelming abundance right now. So instead, I glared at the floor, trying to ignore the red-hot lashes and the eyes I could feel grazing over every inch of me.

"Open your legs and rest your hands flat on your thighs," he commanded.

Oh god, why was this happening to me? I knew the consequences all too well now if I didn't obey, but I wasn't just some whore who could spread her legs on demand.

I tried, while every fiber of my body resisted.

Eventually, the will to avoid his belt won out over a lifetime of modesty, and I did what I was told. I obeyed. And I cursed myself for being so weak all the while.

And I sobbed as he looked me over. His expression was neutral, controlled, but I could see the heat blazing in his eyes. It was strange. It was the kind of heated gaze I'd tried to avoid all my life but forced to endure it now, I could analyze it—probably because I couldn't just sit there. I needed to think about something. And not about why he was doing this, or what he was going to do to me next.

So, where did it come from?—that heat? Was he turned on by me?—by something particular about my body? Or would he be just as aroused by any woman, naked and forced to her knees in front of him? And did that same rationale apply to other men, too? So long as a woman played into his fetish, was she interchangeable?

And how did it make me feel? If I could separate myself from my situation, and pretend he was just an ordinary man—an extremely attractive, ordinary man—how would I feel about him looking at me that way?

I didn't like my answer.

"You have a very beautiful body, Pet." He was looking at me expectantly as if he was waiting for me to thank him for the compliment. He really was insane.

He let out a sigh as if he was disappointed, but he seemed to dismiss it. "I'll tend to your welts now. Climb up on the bed and lay down on your stomach."

"My...my backside is fine," I lied, but I'd rather live with the sting for the rest of my life than submit to whatever 'tending' he had in mind.

He eyed me for a moment, maybe debating whether my words constituted disobedience. But I had been careful in my phrasing. I didn't tell him 'no', only that it was unnecessary. Apparently, this coward was a quick learner.

"Suit yourself," he said then, but he proceeded to come even closer. He stopped right in front of me and reached out to stroke his fingers through my hair.

I wanted to pull away, but I held still. There were worse things he could be touching. If I was going to fight him, I was going to save my strength for that. And I knew 'that' was coming. If not now, then soon. I choked back a sob, knowing that in the end, no matter how much I fought him, he would take what he wanted. And whatever he couldn't take, he would just hurt me until I handed it over to him. All it had taken was a few lashes with his belt and I'd jumped to obey. How much more would he take before he was done with me?

An icy chill shivered down my spine at the thought because the answer was clear and far more terrifying than I could have imagined not so long ago. He wanted everything. He wasn't content to rape me and then leave me alone. If that was what he'd wanted, he would have gotten it over with by now. Forcing me to submit, to obey him...he didn't just want my body. He wanted my soul.

It was too bad for him there wasn't much of one left for him to take. But he didn't care—whole or broken, he'd take it all.

"When I return, I expect you to greet me in this position. Always. Do you understand me?"

"Yes," I said, a little too eagerly. But if he was going to return, that also meant he was going to leave. I might still be trapped here, but at least I would be alone.

He chuckled, obviously not missing the eagerness in my tone. But he caressed my cheek once more, and then he was leaving. Across the room, at the door, and then he was gone.

When I heard the scrape of the lock, I breathed a sigh of relief and sprang to my feet. He couldn't damn well make me kneel if he wasn't here, could he? And I wrapped the blanket back around my body, pulling so tight when I tucked the edge between my breasts that it felt like an old-fashioned corset, cinching my breasts together. I didn't care. It felt like armor, and I was glad to have it back on. Exactly how long I'd have it on before he made me take it off again, I didn't know. But I intended to have a better plan than to cry and obey him figured out before he returned.

3
DEREK

"So, how is our lovely, new slave?" Marcos queried as he sat back in the wing-backed leather chair, with one of his more recent acquisitions kneeling at his feet. The girl was plain, certainly nothing like the girl I'd left not long ago in the training room. But this one had submitted quickly and easily under Marcos' guidance, and that was the way he liked it.

And that's the way I usually liked it too, at least as far as work was concerned. Usually. It was easy—breaking something that was so weakly held together it crumbled with the slightest touch. Easy. And boring. Of course, something about it always appealed to me—making something submit, to bend it to my will. How could it not? But it was always unfulfilling in the end.

Now though, after just a few minutes with the fiery, new temptress…it seemed things might get interesting.

"She's more than I could have hoped for," I replied honestly, thinking Marcos was missing out with his penchant for the weak-willed and weak-minded.

"I'm glad to hear it, but what I want to know is your assessment of her."

I laughed, but I wasn't surprised. "I think she's not typical of the girls you usually give me, but we knew there was a decent chance of that. She's manageable and I have no doubt it will work out just fine."

He eyed me for a minute, but he let it go at that. The girl wasn't the first atypical slave I'd trained, and she likely wouldn't be the last. Just an interesting and arousing bump in the road.

"So, what do you have planned for her next then?" he queried with a little more interest than usual. Apparently, I wasn't the only one who had noticed the girl was unique.

"Dinner," I said, and it sounded simple enough. I smiled, knowing things were never quite what they seemed.

I rose to leave but then paused. "Has Donovan been informed?"

Marcos glanced at his watch. "Any time now."

Good. There was no backing out now—not that I had any intention of it. With that knowledge, I left the room, going in search of what I would need next.

And ten minutes later, I unlocked the door and wheeled the cart and chair inside. Closing the door behind me, I glanced around, but the girl was nowhere in sight. The shower was running in the other room though, so I had a good idea where she was. And she either hadn't heard me come in or else she'd already forgotten the lesson from just a few hours before.

I left the tray and chair by the door and followed the sound and the billowing steam into the bathroom, but the scene wasn't what I'd expected. It was strange enough to think she'd decided to grab a shower so soon, but she wasn't even in the shower. She stood just a few feet from it, wrapped in the damn blanket I should have taken with me. She was barely visible through the steam, but as I got closer, I saw the moisture glistening on her skin. She'd turned the room into a fucking sauna. Did she think this was a day at the spa?

"What are you doing?" I asked, keeping my tone light, amused.

She whirled around, startled to find me there so close behind her. The look of panic and indecision on her face was priceless, but it did seem that what I'd told her before I left had slipped her mind. That, or she was a glutton for punishment—not that I minded.

She remained there on her feet, staring back at me defiantly, though I could see the way her lower jaw trembled. I cocked an eyebrow, giving her one last chance to use some common sense.

She didn't take it.

She squared her shoulders and lifted her chin higher, but it had none of the desired effects when her whole body was trembling with fear. It was amusing though. Almost cute. Like one of those pint-sized dogs barking at a pit bull.

The pint-sized pup didn't know it, but everyone else could plainly see that the pit bull could rip it to shreds without breaking a sweat.

"So, you've decided to be difficult, have you? I can be difficult too, Pet," I said as I reached for her.

She pulled her arm out of reach and tried to sidestep me. But not only was I stronger than her, I was faster too. I grabbed hold of her around the waist and yanked off the damn blanket—and made a mental note to take the thing with me this time. And then I dragged her out of the bathroom to the bed.

I shackled her wrists to the restraints protruding from the mattress and her whole body stiffened in anticipation of what she thought was about to come.

Shame on me if I was ever that predictable.

I chuckled and left her there while I went to retrieve the cart and chair I'd brought in, and I pulled them over next to her, just out of her reach. She tried to angle her body away from me, which only emphasized her slender curves. She was scared, no doubt still waiting for the lash of the belt, but she was also clearly confused. Good.

I removed the lid from the tray and breathed in deep. As always, the food was exquisite. And by the way she stilled, she was beginning to realize what was going on. She'd lost several hours unconscious on the trip here, and then several more since then. While her mind wasn't fully cognizant of the time that had passed, her body was becoming abruptly aware that nearly twenty-four hours had gone by since she'd last eaten.

"I had intended to be kind, to reward your obedience. I was going to feed you, Pet. You are hungry, aren't you?"

She glared at me, but her nostrils flared, taking in the delicious aroma.

"Answer me," I growled.

"Y-yes."

"Yes, what?"

"Yes...I'm hungry."

"And after the fit, you threw—after you

disobeyed me—do you think I should feed you?"

"Yes," she barked.

"Is that so? Then what would stop you from disobeying me again?" I took a bite of the food on the plate.

She squeezed her lips together. She refused to beg for forgiveness, and of course, she was stubborn, so she couldn't agree with me.

I took another bite and another. Her stomach growled, but to her credit, she didn't make a sound, and she barely moved a muscle. Only her eyes moved, following the fork from the plate to my mouth, over and over again. Even when she could see that the last few bites were going fast, she held strong.

When all the food was gone, her shoulders slumped just a little. I'd been hoping she would have put her pride aside for the sake of basic human survival, but I couldn't say I was actually disappointed. It was just too much fun to watch the exquisite girl battle it out in her head. She was most certainly shaping up to be the challenge I'd hoped for.

I re-covered the tray with the lid and wheeled it to the door and out of the room. While I'd debated leaving her shackled there, I couldn't help but think of the steamy scene I'd walked in on, and I was curious what she would do next if left unshackled and to her own devices. I left the chair, too, just to add something new to the mix.

As I approached her, she slunk back, still anticipating the spanking that wouldn't come —at least, not yet. I caressed her cheek when she could slink no further away. She had incredibly soft skin, and I couldn't deny that I was more than a little tempted to keep touching her just to feel her silken flesh beneath my fingers.

I could see it in her eyes when she started to debate whether to sink her teeth into my hand. I'd seen Vito's hand—her teeth were a powerful weapon, indeed—but she thought better of it and kept her lips clamped shut.

That was a good sign. She could have easily done it—at least, she would have thought she could—but she already feared the consequences of such a reckless action. Stubborn, but not stupid. I was liking my new slave more every minute.

Without a word, I unshackled her wrists, half-expecting her to lunge at me with teeth bared. But she didn't move. She eyed me warily as I turned away, and I could feel her eyes boring into my back as I strode out of the room.

I adjusted my cock once I'd closed the door. The girl was the most appealing sight I could remember, but we were just getting started.

I sighed, thinking of the slaves Marcos kept in the house. I could use one now to take the edge off, but somehow it seemed like a poor substitute for what I had in store.

When I returned in the morning and wheeled in the tray laden with food, I was only half-surprised to find her in the bathroom again. The water in the shower was running but there was no steam billowing out into the other room this time. Either she was running it on cold, or else she'd left it running for so many hours that the hot water had run out.

I felt an odd pang when I went to investigate and found her huddled in the corner with her knees drawn up and her head tilted to the side. She was asleep, but the tears she'd cried had dried on her cheeks. Beneath the fan of her eyelids, the delicate skin was darker, the result of a combination of fatigue and a lack of food.

Her hair was dry though, suggesting she hadn't made use of the shower. But then, why did she have it running? It was odd, and it made me curious, but there would be time enough for answers. Right now, she needed to abandon her hard-headedness for the sake of her health.

"Wake up," I said, none too gently. I wasn't there to hold her hand.

She startled awake, but she remained where she was, huddled in the corner.

"You've been a fool and you're suffering unnecessarily. I'm done tolerating it. Kneel. Now."

She acquiesced more readily than I'd expected, though fatigue and hunger could do a lot to one's resolve—I would know.

Her shoulders were slumped and her arms hung limply over her body in a half-hearted attempt to cover herself.

Her fatigue was too pronounced. Something wasn't right.

"When was the last time you ate?" I asked, beginning to suspect the cause.

She stared blankly at the floor.

"When?" I demanded.

"Last...last night. At dinner. At home," she replied quietly.

But that wasn't right—her sense of time would have been distorted, so I had to extrapolate what that really meant. Dinner—at home. The last time she'd been home was the morning before her shift on the day she'd been taken. And dinner at home meant the night before that. And that meant when she'd stubbornly refused to submit when I'd come with food yesterday evening, she'd already gone forty-eight hours without food. And now, twelve hours later, the fool had gone somewhere around sixty hours without food.

I was very particular in the taking of any new girl. She was to be surveilled, and every aspect of the day leading up to the event recorded for me. Vito had reported that she'd eaten at the store where she worked just prior to her leaving work. If the girl was telling the truth though—which by her physical state, it suggested she was—it meant Vito had lied to me. No doubt, he'd lied to punish the girl for biting him. But I didn't give a fuck what his god damned reason was. The son of a bitch had lied. To me. And I'd make sure he didn't make that mistake twice.

For now, though, I had the problem in front of me to rectify. I turned off the shower and retrieved the cart from the other room, actually wheeling it right into the bathroom. The girl needed food, and I wasn't going to risk her defying me further and having to withhold it.

With an air of nonchalance, I removed the lid from the tray and proceeded to cut up the food. I shoved a forkful in front of her lips, half-expecting to have to force it into her mouth. But her lips parted and she snatched the food off, chewing greedily. And too fast.

"Slowly," I cautioned, and filled the fork again, though with half as much food this time.

She devoured the entire plate, though it took quite a bit of time since I started to insist she wait in between bits, in part to make her wait, and partly because a stomach that empty could turn quickly—another fact I knew all too well.

I left when she was done, fully expecting her next feeding to go smoothly after getting past this first battle.

But I'd expected too much. With her body no longer weak from starvation, the fire in her reignited. She was in her corner in the bathroom with the shower running again when I returned, but the moment I walked in, the stubborn light shined bright in her eyes.

I didn't relish the idea of leaving her with no food—she really did need it after so much time without. But when she glared back at me when I told her to kneel, she left me with no choice. So, I held off on dinner as long as I could and wheeled the cart right into the bathroom—where I knew she would be.

"Kneel," I said, letting my fingers hover over the belt around my waist.

She glared at me, but she also did what she was told—a fucking miracle, given the same stubborn light had flashed in her eyes. It seemed then, with the way she'd moved quickly after the threat of the belt, that she feared physical discipline more than starvation. And that meant a firm hand would be what this one needed.

And I was more than happy to accommodate that need.

4

SCARLETT

I had no idea how many days passed. There was no way for me to keep track—no clock, no window to see outside. Nothing. But what I did know with increasing certainty was I had winded up straight in hell. The man who kept bringing me food, making me kneel like an animal at his feet and spanking my backside with a hard slap whenever I hesitated—he was the devil himself. He was cruel, and worst of all, the thing I hated most was that he left me alone in my prison with nothing but the god damned silence.

I couldn't stand it. No sounds of cars in the distance or birds chirping outside. Not even footsteps or the low murmur of voices to suggest I was anything other than completely alone.

I'd debated provoking him over and over again, just to give him a reason to stay, a reason to talk. Hell, the sound of his breathing was better than the utter nothingness that surrounded me when he left.

During some meals, he would ask me things, questions like my favorite book and my favorite movie, and so long as I handed over whatever he wanted to know, he kept asking questions, staving off the silence I knew was coming. But the moment he ventured into personal territory and I refused to answer, he left. And the world was silent again.

The shower helped a little. At least, it did at first. But an hour or two of the monotonous sound of running water and it seemed to blur right into the nothingness. I couldn't keep going like this. It was going to drive me mad.

Maybe that's what he was trying to do. At first, when those men had stripped me and the devil had spanked me with his belt, I'd assumed what he wanted was sexual in nature. But now, even though I was forced to remain naked all the time, I wasn't so sure. In the times he was here, feeding me like a dog and making my blood boil with anger and humiliation, I thought maybe what he wanted was a pet. But then he'd leave and wouldn't return until it was time to feed me again. Who the hell only wanted a pet to feed it?

So, all I could conclude was that he was merely feeding me to keep me alive so he could watch me slowly go insane.

It was almost time for another feeding. I could tell by the way my stomach had begun to rumble. He must come at regular intervals to have my stomach so well-trained. It irritated me that any part of me had come to submit to him, but my stomach had willingly gotten on board that train.

No other part of me had though. It was still a humiliating struggle every time to go down on my knees, to open my mouth and let him feed me like an infant. The worst was when he did touch me, not sexually—aside from swatting my backside, he never did that—but intimately.

He would stroke my hair or caress my cheek. And what made it so horrible was that not once had I ever pulled away. His touch felt...good and I hated that. But after so much time with no sound, no new sights, no anything, my body seemed desperate for sensation. And the touch of my captor's hand against my face was better than the nothingness. I was ashamed to admit it, but there were times when I'd secretly wished he'd touch me more, in new places. A hand on my arm, or his fingers on the back of my neck—new sensations to hold me over during the times when there was none.

Still, I wanted to scream at him—for humiliating me, for touching me, for not touching me, for asking me things and never sharing any answers of his own—and I nearly had so many times, but I held myself in check, knowing at any time he could stop coming back. The food would be gone and I'd starve to death. Much longer here though, and that might not be such a terrible thing.

I heard the slide of the lock and the door opened. It was him. Of course, it was him. Nobody else in the world existed anymore, not in my prison. I was irritated—more than usual—probably due to the compounding effect of so much time here.

He wheeled in the cart and closed the door behind him, and I watched him from the corner of the room. I'd long since abandoned the bathroom. The shower did little to curb the silence anymore. And at least the other room's carpet wasn't as hard against my backside as the cool, tiled floor in the bathroom.

I'd thought for a while I could gauge the approximate time of day by the type of food he would bring, but then he'd brought breakfast two times in a row, and two dinner-like meals after that, blowing that theory out of the water. It was the same foods though—three different meals rotated in some random order.

Crepes again, I could tell, when he'd lifted the lid. Maybe it was all he could cook, but I'd gladly take a peanut butter and jelly sandwich for a break from what had once seemed like sinfully delicious food.

He left the tray against the wall near the door and retrieved the chair from where he'd left it the day before. This was new.

He sat down against the wall and eyed me expectantly. I pushed away from my corner slowly and rose up onto my knees.

He nodded, but I was confused. If he planned to start throwing food at me and having me catch it in my mouth, he could kiss that idea goodbye. It was bad enough I had to kneel. I wasn't going to do tricks, too. And as much as I hated to admit it, if he was going to stay over there, if he was going to stop touching me, I'd rather him just stop bringing me food, too.

I'd never imagined how dependent on sensation I was, especially when the only consistent in my life—my father—never touched me. He didn't hug me, or pat me on the back. He never kissed me good night. But there were always at least other sensations—the sound of his TV murmuring the news or some cheesy sitcom; the smell of the alcohol he drank or the pungent aroma of his cigarettes.

And then at work, there were other sensations—people talking, the photo machine whirring, the scent of perfumes, colognes, and food from the restaurant down the street. There were children to watch playing along the sidewalk and the brush of the breeze against my skin when I walked home.

Here, there was nothing. If there had ever been

a scent in the room, I'd long-since acclimated to it. And there was nothing else. No people, no sounds, no scents. There wasn't even a single book to read.

My books—I missed my books. I had hundreds of them, most of them passed on to me from customers in the store, like Mrs. Jenkins, who forever saw me with my nose in a book. Mysteries, romances, crime thrillers, biographies, even an old nursing textbook from Mrs. Jenkin's college years. What I wouldn't give for any one of them now.

But the only sensation I was allowed was my captor's brief touch. I hated him; I hated him even more for making me crave something I despised, but I did crave it. If it was gone now, if he wasn't even going to touch me during the brief time he was here, then it was only fair he put me out of my misery—not that I expected him to be fair.

"Come here," he called, startling me out of my dark thoughts. I hesitated for a moment, but if it meant we could circumvent the whole trick-performing plan and he wasn't intending to deprive me of the sensation I desperately needed, then it probably wasn't so bad.

I moved to stand, but he shook his head and I stopped. What did he want then? It didn't take me long to figure it out. Kneeling was no longer enough. He wanted me to crawl.

No. I wasn't that hungry, and it really was ridiculous to be so dependent on his touch. And if he retaliated by making me skip a few meals, I'd get over it. And I'd find some way to deal with it when he took away his touch, too.

So, I lifted my chin higher and shook my head.

He sighed and stood up. I thought he was going to bring over the tray of food or else leave, but he approached without it.

"I have been more than patient," he said when he stood in front of me. "I've been lenient, giving you the opportunity to make the necessary changes to your character on your own. But you're not going to do that, are you, Pet?"

Necessary changes? Of course, I wasn't going to change for him. Had he really thought I would? I shook my head, apparently not quite brave enough to spit out the words.

"That's what I thought," he said with a sigh. It sounded like a sigh of relief though, not resignation, and that confused me.

Before I could respond, he yanked me up off the floor and flung me over his shoulder. As he started toward the bed, I realized I'd been foolish to let myself forget about that first day with him, when he'd pulled off his belt and spanked me with it, shackled to the bed. Is that what he had planned to do now?

But when he reached the bed, he didn't put me on the floor like I'd expected. Instead, he sat down and pulled me into his lap. I struggled weakly to escape, but I was so confused I didn't really know what to do. He held me tight with one arm while the other stroked my cheek, and I sighed inside. A change from the nothingness. I welcomed it, though I was careful to keep my expression from showing it.

After a moment though, I couldn't help but lean into it, absorbing the sensation after too much time without. But this new position made me painfully aware of my state of undress, somehow more potent now on his lap than it had been on the floor.

"I knew it wouldn't be enough, Pet, but I had to give you this time to realize you're never going to become what you need to be without my help."

What I needed to be? What was he talking about? Somehow I doubted anything he could do could be constituted as help.

"You have to let go of this stubbornness and pride," he said as he continued to stroke my cheek, and then moving lower, across my jaw, down to my neck.

My body hummed in response to the new sensation. He hadn't touched me there before, and it seemed to awaken a plethora of nerve endings. Through my haze of sensation bliss—as wrong as it might be—I was vaguely aware of his words. The tone of his voice was soothing, particularly heaped upon the touch of his fingers, but there was an undercurrent running through him that was slowly breaking through the haze. I knew somehow that it should be setting me more on edge than usual.

And then there was an expectant silence as if he was waiting for me to say something. Was I supposed to apologize? Agree with him? Did he really think I was going to do either? I sat there stiffly, trying to ignore the sensations that came from where he was touching me.

"All right, let's get started, shall we?" he said, leaving me just as confused as I'd been since the moment he'd come in and sat down across the room.

All of a sudden though, he flipped me over, laying me out on his lap. I flailed, trying to scramble down onto the floor, but he held me tight against him, pressing the small of my back down firmly, which pressed my most private place hard against his thigh. A sizzle of a different kind of sensation spread out from there, and I flailed harder, twice as panicked, and infinitely more disturbed than I'd been when my body had responded to his touch on my face or even my neck.

But he just pressed down harder, almost as if he was deliberately trying to grind my clit against his thigh. And whether it was intentional or not, that was precisely what he was doing, and I needed him to stop. It was wrong. Disgusting. How could my body be responding like this to anything he did?

I felt his other hand against my backside, grazing over my skin. It amplified the sensations between my thighs and made me want to press firmly against his hand. I sobbed at my own depravity. What the hell was wrong with me? What had I become in my desperate need for sensation?

His hand disappeared and I let out a small sigh of relief. But before the breath had escaped my lungs, his hand came back down with a stinging slap.

I cried out in response to the pain, and to something else. It was sick, and it made me question if I'd already taken a leap into insanity. There was no other explanation for it. How else could it be possible that his cruel slap could send a jolt of arousal through me?

He spanked me again, this one harder than the last, but the response was the same.

Again, and tears began to trickle down my cheeks. I clenched my thighs tight, fighting against the ridiculous sensations that had begun to set my sex on fire. "Stop. Please, stop," I cried, but he ignored me, spanking me several more times in quick succession.

I struggled to get away, but it only rubbed my clit against his thigh, making it worse. So, I fought to remain perfectly still as he rained down another onslaught of stinging slaps.

It didn't help. The fire had already been set. Nothing would put it out, and every slap and every rub only made it burn brighter. What the hell was wrong with me?

Eventually, he was done—twenty-five slaps? Thirty? Every one of them had added fuel to the fire, and now I was throbbing, desperate for anything that would quench the fire.

Instead of pushing me off, he held me there and rubbed my stinging flesh. The need to press myself harder against him was nearly overwhelming. I took slow, deep breaths, but somehow the oxygen in my lungs wound its way through my body to between my thighs and fanned the flames brighter.

His fingers skimmed down the backs of my thighs—a new sensation that shot directly to my throbbing clit. But on his way back up, he brushed over my exposed sex and his fingers stopped moving.

I redoubled the effort to get free, but his hand on my back held me there.

One finger stroked me, and I sobbed hysterically. His finger had glided far too easily, and that meant there was no denying what his spanking had done to me.

"You are very unique, aren't you, Pet," he said as he glided back and forth across my lips.

"Let me go. Please, just let me go," I cried over and over again, but of course, he ignored me. His torment wouldn't be complete until he'd turned my whole body against me.

He slid a finger to my clit and my body jerked against him. No matter how much I flailed, or how much I didn't want my body to respond, I was helpless to stop it as he started to rub the sensitive bundle of nerves. He moved slowly at first as if he were testing my body's response.

I kicked and tried to reach back to swipe at him, but all I met with was air. He knew exactly what he was doing because he had me pinned perfectly. His finger increased its pace on my clit and I couldn't stifle the moan that traitorously escaped from my lips.

He chuckled, and I couldn't possibly have been more mortified. He found it amusing, the way my body had betrayed me.

"Stop resisting, Pet. It will be over quicker if you don't fight it."

I knew what he was saying was true. All my effort was doing little more than slowing my body's ascent. Unless he stopped, it was going to happen soon. I could feel the coil winding up tight inside me. But I couldn't just stop. I couldn't be a willing participant in my own humiliation.

So, I continued to fight him, clenching my body and gritting my teeth against the spin of the coil, winding faster, tighter by the second.

He increased his pace even more, determined to overcome my resistance, and I almost gave in. God, how I wanted to give in. The sensations were overwhelming, the first bit of real pleasure since I'd ended up in this wretched place.

He moved faster, his finger gliding easily, soaked in my own juices. I was so close. So damn close. No. Yes. No. No! I had to fight. But as I neared the top, my body took over. It refused to fight, to resist. All that existed was his finger on my clit. But then his other hand was on my ass, squeezing my stinging flesh. God, it hurt, and it felt so good as if the pain and pleasure had combined to create a new sensation—one I hadn't known existed.

I writhed against him, and the moans I'd fought so hard against turned to cries. "Please," I cried, but I wasn't begging him to stop. I was pleading for something else, for the release that hovered on the brink.

And then I was toppling over. I'd asked, and he'd delivered, springing free the coil that had wound tight inside me and sending out waves of blissful pleasure from my sex.

I sagged against him as the waves receded, and only realized then that with his hand on my backside, that meant he hadn't been holding me down. I could have scrambled away, but I hadn't. I'd laid there, writhing, on fire and begging for the orgasm he'd given me.

I did scramble down off his lap then, and he didn't stop me. I ran across the room to the corner—my corner.

He didn't demand that I come back. He didn't even laugh at me like I'd been expecting him to do. In fact, he seemed to ignore me completely as he turned his attention to the tray of food. He seemed relaxed as he sliced the food and began to eat, but there was a tension that radiated from him, all the way across the room.

It wasn't anger—what did he have to be angry about? He'd humiliated me more than I thought was possible for a person to be. He was probably quite pleased with himself at the moment. Still, the tension remained through bite after bite, and eventually, I recognized it. I couldn't not. Not when it had been the same tension that had held my body in its grip when he'd had his wretched fingers on me. Spanking me, or turning my body against me, or some combination of both had turned him on.

Without my permission, my eyes darted to the fly of his pants, looking for confirmation. And the massive bulge I found there left no doubt.

So, this was sexual for him. Then why had he spent so much time tormenting me with silence? I'd dismissed the possibility after what must have been days of near-total solitude. And it wasn't that I wanted it—I didn't want this to be sexual, no matter how much my body had just proved otherwise. But I needed to understand, to know what exactly my future held in store. Or maybe I just needed to think about something—anything—other than how my body had just turned against me and responded to the devil's touch just moments before. Trying desperately to fight back more tears, it was easier to try to analyze him than to turn the looking glass inward.

It dawned on me then what he was doing. He was eating my food. When it was gone, there would be no more until he returned. And I had run back to the very spot this had started. If I wanted food, I would have to crawl over to him —to the man who had taken humiliation to a whole new level—and kneel before him like a good pet. But I couldn't do that. I wouldn't. I didn't want to see the knowledge in his eyes of what I'd let happen.

No, I would rather starve.

He finished my meal while I huddled in the corner. I tried not to look at him, but sick curiosity kept drawing my eyes back. I'd never seen one before—the thick bulge in his pants. I'd seen drawings in health class and had learned that a penis increased in size when a man was aroused. But I'd never imagined it could grow that much.

Against my will, the image came to mind of him trying to force that enormous bulge inside me. I cringed, thinking I would certainly split in two. But the thought appealed to the sick, depraved girl inside me, the one who had writhed against his fingers and moaned in pleasure despite how wrong it was.

What the hell had he done to me? Before this, I'd never...well...there'd been the occasional strange dream, the kind that would wake me, sweaty and aching, and disgusted with myself for conjuring the dark scenes.

But they had been dreams—nightmares by any normal standard. And this was reality—bitter, harsh reality. I couldn't simply wake up from this nightmare and shame-facedly relieve the ache before drifting back to an innocent slumber. But maybe that's all this was. My body was simply responding the way it had in those dreams. I'd rewarded it often enough for it, rubbing hard and fast to the last snatches of the dream until my body convulsed with its relief.

It didn't make it any less humiliating now, but it helped to explain why I'd responded the way I had.

"You are very unique, Pet," he said, drawing my attention back as he rose from the chair. And then he left with the tray.

I debated going to check around the chair, pathetically hoping he'd left some kind of scraps behind, but I knew he hadn't. It would be hours before I had the chance to eat again, and who knew what horrible thing he'd make me do for it.

It seemed I no longer paid for things with money—of which I'd had precious little, to begin with. The price he demanded was my pride. My humiliation bought me food, but what happened when he'd extracted every bit of it from me? Then what would he demand in payment?

I closed my eyes and shifted tighter into my corner. The carpet rubbed against my abused bottom, providing a fresh reminder of what had happened and making the tears in my eyes well over. Maybe it would be better to get it over with—to stop resisting, stop trying to hold onto the pride and dignity he was just going to take away from me in the end.

I'd been right about this being sexual for him. And I'd been right that he'd been trying to slowly drive me insane. I had a feeling he wasn't going to stop until he turned the girl he'd taken into nothing but a complacent shell he could use any way he wanted. Why try to stop it from happening when it was going to happen eventually?

I breathed a deep sigh, trying to cleanse the fight from my body. It held on tight. I could feel it wrapped tight around somewhere in the center of me, woven into the fabric of my being. I kept breathing, trying to disentangle each strand.

My eyes grew heavy, and I didn't fight them. Every moment of sleep had been a struggle, but now it seemed like the exhaustion had finally caught up with me. I welcomed it, willing it to help me slip away. To escape the pain, the uncertainty, the humiliation...even if only for a little while. I would struggle to offer it all up later. I would worry about handing over whatever pride I had left later. Later.

I drifted off quickly, but he followed me there. In my dream, he teased and tormented me. He tied me up and he hurt me. And he held me down with my arms pinned above my head and he rammed his massive cock deep inside me.

When I awoke, I was sweaty, and the aching throb between my thighs was all too familiar.

But when I looked up, he was there. He was staring down at me with an amused grin on his too-handsome face. My cheeks flamed, remembering the scene in my dream and wondering what clues my sleeping body had given him about what had been going on in my head. Had I moaned? Begged? Touched myself?

"Hello, Pet. Sweet dreams?" he queried with an expression that said he knew too much. "Kneel," he said and I struggled up onto my knees, hoping he'd abandon the subject and feed me. I'd gladly crawl all around the room if he'd just leave the topic alone.

Instead, though, he crouched down in front of me and he slipped his hand between my thighs.

I tried to back up, but my corner gave me nowhere to go.

He didn't run his fingers along me this time but shoved a finger inside me. Oh god. Sensation. Too damn much sensation. On top of the dream that still clung to my body, his touch was too much.

"Hmm, very sweet dreams it seems," he said as he removed his finger and raised it to his lips.

My wetness glistened on his finger and I squeezed my eyes shut as he slipped it into his mouth. And then I felt him pressing his finger against my lips, trying to force it inside. I kept them closed until a low growl rumbled up from his chest in warning. Reluctantly, I let him in, and I tasted myself on the invading digit. It wasn't crepes, or either of the other meals he fed me. It was something different. New. Earthy, with a soft sweetness like honey. The new sensation fed my depraved brain.

"Tell me about your dream," he persisted.

"I-I don't want to," I said, finding it difficult to

concoct some mundane dream with the man who'd starred in it in front of me and my body taut with unwelcome arousal.

"You know what you want is irrelevant," He told me. "You can tell me, or you can fight me on it and I'll strap you to the bed and whip you until you do."

Something told me he wasn't bluffing. "You," I blurted out. "...you were inside me," I confessed miserably.

He looked surprised—I'd actually surprised him—but it was short-lived. "If you wanted me to fuck you, Pet, why didn't you just say so?" he asked, but he was just taunting me. Even if I did want it—which I didn't—if I had asked him for it, he would have denied me just to torment me more.

"I-I don't."

"I don't think your body agrees with you," He said as he slipped his finger back inside me. I tried to squirm away. I really did try. Or at least, I wanted to. But it felt so good; like a thousand sensations all at once. Besides, it would make no difference. If I shot to my feet and tried to get away, he'd just stop me and punish me for it. Maybe if I stayed still, he'd tire of me.

But he kept it up, plunging in shallowly, again and again, making my body clench around him innately, trying to draw him in deeper. And then he did. He thrust in deeper, and his finger glided against too many sensitive nerve endings for me to stop the quiet moan that escaped my lips. But then he froze, right there inside me.

I wanted to run, and I wanted to make him move inside me, both wants warring against each other and keeping me just as frozen in place.

"You're a virgin?" he asked, though it sounded more like a statement than a question. However, the surprise in his eyes was unmistakable.

"Y-yes," I sobbed, knowing that if there'd been any hope of him leaving that part of me alone, it had just vanished.

"You're nearly twenty years old. And you look like this," he said, motioning to my body with the hand that hadn't stilled inside me. "How's that possible."

I didn't want to like what he was saying. I didn't want to take it as a compliment, that he thought I was attractive. It shouldn't matter. It didn't matter. And yet, a small, despicable thrill traveled through me, realizing it was true.

But he wanted to know how it was possible I was still virgin? Maybe because I'd spent every day of my life since becoming a teenager trying in vain to prove I wasn't a whore, that I would never be a whore. Not like my mother. Every day I spent trying to show my father I wasn't like her.

But it turned out...I was just like her. There was no denying it now, now when all I wanted to focus on was the finger inside me, the finger that I desperately wanted to start moving again, preferably back to my clit like he'd been doing before, rubbing until the fire inside me culminated into something exquisite.

He didn't though. He moved around inside me as if just enough to make sure I didn't forget that he was there—as if I could. And then, all of a sudden, he withdrew completely and stood up. I didn't watch where he went—it was too humiliating to look up, and I didn't want to see what he was doing. I kept my eyes glues to a speck of fluff on the floor by my feet.

He returned a moment later, and I wished I'd paid better attention—not that it would have made any difference in the outcome. He hauled me to my feet and shackled my wrists in the restraints that must have been the ones attached to the bed. I tried to pull away, but of course, it was useless.

He pulled me over to the bed and hooked the restraints high up on one of the posts, which pressed hard against my face and the valley between my breasts. Had I made him angry? Why was he doing this?

But when I turned my head to look at him, he didn't look angry. "What are you doing?" I whispered frantically.

"You've been full of surprises, Pet, and I think I'd like some answers," he explained. "This is how it works. I'm going to ask you a question. When you tell me the truth, I will reward you with pleasure. For every time I believe you have lied to me, you will get the belt. Do you understand?"

No! Of course, I didn't understand any of it. But I kept my mouth shut and nodded once. What difference did it make? He'd do what he wanted regardless of whether I understood.

"Good. Let's get started then," he said as he reached around from behind me and palmed my breasts. I tried to wriggle out of his hands but stretched tautly, I couldn't move more than an inch. And even if I had been able to get away, would I have? The fire between my thighs was anything but extinguished and what he was doing was feeding it. Would I have stopped him, even if I'd been able to? Not so long ago, I would have said yes, with absolute certainty. But it was harder to believe that now when I could feel my chest straining against the post between my breasts, trying to press harder into his hands.

"Have you ever let a man do this, Pet?" he asked as he toyed with my nipples, sending rivulets of desire to my sex.

"N-no," I answered honestly.

"Really? And what about this?" he persisted as his hands grazed down to my backside and cupped my cheeks.

"No..." I answered as the pulsating between my legs intensified.

"What about this?" One hand circled around in front. "Have you ever let a man play with your hot, little pussy?" His fingers pressed against my clit and started to rub.

"No...never," I whispered, certain I was red with embarrassment from head to toe.

"You have a beautiful body, and you've kept it to yourself your entire life—why?"

I didn't want to answer. It wasn't just my body or my pride he was after, but my secrets, the things that made up who I was. But what would be a feasible reason? Why did a normal girl abstain from sex?

"I just...I'm not good with people. I'm awkward, that's all." Yes, it made sense. A socially awkward girl would have a hard time getting a date.

"I didn't ask why you don't have a boyfriend. I want to know why you don't fuck."

"It's the same thing!" I yelled and then tried to

rein it in. "I mean...I couldn't just go up to some guy on the street and...you know..."

He chuckled. "Actually yes, Pet, you really could."

He meant it. He really thought I was attractive enough that I could do that. I hated how much I liked hearing that. He rubbed faster, making my body jerk against him.

"But you lied to me, didn't you?" His tone had grown serious.

How could he know that? He couldn't possibly know the reason I'd done my best to be a good girl, to be anything but what he was turning me into.

He stopped rubbing, and I heard the quiet slide of his belt as he slipped it off his pants. "No, please. Don't," I cried.

The belt landed with a thwack across my backside, and it jolted my whole body, pressing my clit hard against the post directly in front of me, and making my body respond with a fiery ache. Oh god, no. Not this, too.

Another lash, crisscrossing the first. It stung,

making me cry out, but it made the fire in me blaze hotter, too.

Two more, and then he dropped the belt on the bed in front of me. "Let's try this again. Why?" he asked as he ran his fingers lightly over where he'd struck me.

"Because of my father," I sobbed. "Because he always said I'd be a whore." Now was he satisfied? He'd wrenched that private piece from me.

He didn't move for a moment, as if he was taking time to process what I'd said. I thought he was done—he'd gotten his answers. I needed him to leave. I needed to be alone, and as much as I hated to admit it, I desperately needed to quench the fire he'd created that was making it near-impossible to think about anything else.

But then he reached around me and his fingers made contact with my too-sensitive flesh. I moaned—I couldn't stop it. And something inside me snapped.

I'd confessed. I'd admitted out loud what had dictated my life for so long. But with the admission came the acceptance that I'd failed. The way my body was burning, the years of dark and twisted dreams, and the thoughts running through my head right now of just what I wanted this man—my captor—to do to my body.

Whatever he'd done to me had vanquished a lifetime of keeping my body and thoughts in check. And what I hated most, what made me wish I could wrap my hands around his neck and strangle him to death, was that it felt so damn good. To thrust harder against his fingers and feel him rubbing faster. And faster. To feel him driving me higher.

There was no sense in denying it. He knew exactly what he was doing to me. He knew what I was, how my body responded in ways it shouldn't. He knew I was the whore I'd tried to deny being for too long.

And I didn't care. I didn't want him to stop.

"Oh god, yes," I cried when I was nearly there. I didn't want to bite back the words, or the moans. And I didn't want to stop my body from writhing against him. I'd kept it locked up all my life, and my only reward for it was this hell, this devil.

God damn it, I just wanted to come. If he was going to make my life a living hell, then I was going to take what pleasure from it I could.

And when I was there, when I'd reached the brink, I didn't try to stop it. I threw myself over the edge as wave upon wave of depraved pleasure pulsed through me.

"Very good, Pet," he whispered next to my ear as I came back down.

The intensity of my arousal now past, what I'd done, how I'd spurred it on was like a thousand drops of humiliation all raining down on me in the aftermath.

"Unfortunately, why you've kept your pussy to yourself is not the only lie you told, is it?"

"I don't know what you're talking about," I sobbed. I really didn't.

"You said you've never let a man play with your pussy. But you let me, didn't you?" he whispered slyly as he reached for the belt.

I opened my mouth to protest, but remembering the way I'd welcomed his touch, not just now but the last time as well when he'd spanked me, I slammed it closed. But I yanked hard on the restraints at the same time, trying futilely to escape.

He couldn't do this. He was the one who'd made my body respond like that. I hadn't wanted it. It wasn't my fault. And my fault or not, with my body's arousal sated and my backside still stinging from his belt, this was only going to hurt. Badly.

"Stop. No. Don't," I yelled, but it didn't faze him.

He brought the belt down with another resounding thwack, and the pain radiated down to my toes.

Again, but this time there was something else in the pain, a kindling spark.

One more, and when the lash of fire jerked my hips forward and pressed my clit against the post, I held myself there, feeling the spark burst into a flame. It was depraved and mortifying, but it was also the only way to turn the pain into something else, something even hotter than the fiery sting of my backside.

Two more, and I started to rub wantonly

against the post. I couldn't stop what he was doing to me, but I could use it. I could use my body's sick pleasure to escape the pain.

He dropped the belt after two more strikes, and when he reached up to the restraints, I thought he was finally finished with me.

But again, I was wrong.

He spun me around until I was facing him and hooked the restraints there. I was breathing heavy, but not out of my mind with arousal, still sane enough that I tried to object when he knelt down in front of me and lifted my foot off the ground. When he lowered it onto his shoulder, I tried to yank it away, but he held it firm. And then he leaned in until he was just a hair's breadth away.

I could fight him—not that it would amount to anything. I could feel his warm breath on my moist flesh. Did I want to fight him?

As if my body was answering for itself, my hips jerked forward and his mouth pressed against my clit. I could hear him chuckling, but then his tongue flicked across the sensitive nub, and I didn't care.

He flicked back and forth, fast, and my body started to writhe. I felt the oddest need to touch him—to feel his flesh beneath my fingers, to twine them in his hair and hold him close against my sex. But handcuffed, all I could do was stand there and watch as his mouth did wicked things, flicking, sucking and nipping at me until the world narrowed once more to his mouth and the wildfire he was feeding with everything he did.

When he sent me over the edge this time, I could feel the blissful waves of my orgasm from my fingertips to the tips of my toes.

He looked up at me, his lips glistening, but it wasn't his lips that caught my attention. It was his eyes. Vivid, blue eyes. Comforting eyes in a man who was anything but a comfort. Why? And why did they seem so god damned familiar?

He stood, and I waited for him to mock me, or touch me, or spank me, or whatever else he had in mind. But he just unshackled me and left. He walked out of the room without a word.

5
DEREK

She was beyond exquisite. Hell, I couldn't put a name to what she was. Her unique response to being touched, to being disciplined was beyond arousing, and it meant she might just be ready for sale a whole lot earlier than I'd expected. The revenge I'd sought, craved, for years, it was within my grasp now. Though she was stubborn, her innate desires and the way she seemed to despise them would help to break her down.

When I'd first laid eyes on her, I'd thought it might have taken months to make her ready, but there was no way I could have known what was lurking beneath the surface. And just four weeks in, she would be ready in a few more weeks at most.

The problem was, the last thing I wanted to do was give her away—a problem I'd never encountered before. Even back when Marcos had introduced me to training slaves, I was always anxious to be rid of them, at first out of guilt, and then eventually, out of boredom.

But I wasn't bored, not yet. I was curious though. Sexy, beautiful...and wound up way too tight. She seemed to have genuine difficulties with her sexuality, and that could prove to be a bit of a stumbling block if she held onto it too tight.

But why? Where had they come from? A thought occurred to me, and then it enraged me. I imagined her reluctance had something to do with being forced earlier in life—like by a father. The white, hot rage that coursed through my veins surprised me. To think that her father had used her like that...I already wanted Donovan dead, but right then, death wasn't good enough.

I scoffed at myself—I'd kidnapped her, was in

the process of turning her into a slave, and I was filled with rage over the thought of her father touching her, or making her touch him? That was a new kind of fucked up thinking, even for this monster. But since I couldn't quite get it to calm down enough to bring her dinner, I decided to do a little research, digging up what I could find about how she'd spent the time since being taken from the foster home.

Not much, it turned out—because there wasn't much to tell. I'd located a storage unit in her name before I'd had her abducted, and had the contents brought to me, and that had her apartment inspected after her disappearance. Three boxes. That's all there was. The sum of her life.

I looked through the books at the top of the stack—high school yearbooks. She was there but never smiling. Her eyes were sad, lost like she'd seemed the day I'd watched her. And no one ever wrote in her yearbook. The comments pages were blank.

There was a picture of a woman beneath the yearbooks in the box—a woman who looked very much like her. Her mother, I presumed by the physical similarities. Thinking about it now, the girl looked nothing like James Donovan.

There was only one photo of the woman who had to be her mother, and the picture was worn like it had been handled over and over again for years. I imagined her holding it to her chest every night when she went to bed as a little girl, hiding it underneath her pillow come morning to keep her father from finding it.

There were books—a lot of books. Apparently, she liked to read—a lot. How I knew they weren't her father's, I didn't know, but somehow it fit. With so few friends that her yearbook pages were empty, I imagined she spent a lot of time on her own, reading.

At the bottom of the third box, I found a journal—a locked journal—and it had me curious. So, of course, I broke the lock and looked inside.

A quick scan through showed that it covered several years—from a few months after she'd been taken up until the end of high school.

I felt like I was violating her somehow—ha!—but I looked at the first entry, which was messier than the later ones. She wrote about moving again—the third time since her daddy came to get her. That meant she couldn't have been more than nine or ten years old when she'd written it. She wrote that she didn't like moving so much, but at least it was sometimes better than being in the foster home. Her daddy didn't come into her room at night. In fact, her daddy didn't touch her at all, not like Mr. Vaughan did.

Fuck! I knew that name. I knew it because it was my father's name.

She'd lived with my family for nearly a year. My parents had been good people—I'd thought they'd been good people—taking in foster children as far back as I could remember, and she'd been one of those children.

I re-read the journal entry and then read it again. I couldn't believe what she'd written. It had to be a lie. But what reason did she have to lie in a locked journal that I was quite certain no one else had ever seen? My father had gone into her room at night. He'd touched her—an eight-year-old girl. And I'd had no fucking idea. How many times? What had he done to her?

And how the hell had I never noticed what was going on?

Ignoring the way my blood had begun to boil, I kept reading. And then I wished I hadn't. There was apparently one thing she did miss from her foster care, according to her younger self—me.

"I miss Derek," she'd written bluntly as nine-year-olds were apt to do. "I liked him."

Reading it sent a jolt of something acutely painful through my chest. I could vaguely remember the times the little redhead had bugged to sleep in my room, and I'd told her no, thinking it was the right thing to do. My parents wouldn't have approved, no matter how innocent it was. How many times had I sent her back to her room…to my father?

I felt nauseous and angry, but it was directed inward this time, and I had no idea what to do with it. I should have known, or asked, or done…something. Rage coursed through my veins, and I wanted to hurt the man who'd hurt her, but there wasn't a god damned thing I could do about it. My father was dead and had been for a very long time.

And it was for that death, and for the death of my mother, that I'd been hell-bent on seeking revenge since I was thirteen years old. What the hell was I supposed to do now? Donovan had broken into my home, shot my father point-blank in the forehead, then my mother, and then he'd run out of the house with his daughter beneath his arm.

With no other family, I had been sent to hell, to the care of the vilest people I've ever known. If it hadn't been for Marcos, I would have spent many more years there, locked in a dirty basement, a half-starved punching bag for the asshole and a whore for the bitch.

Was I just supposed to forget about it all because of what my father may or may not have done? Let bygones be bygones? It just wasn't in the repertoire of things I could do.

But for the first time since that horrid night, I hesitated. Maybe Donovan still deserved to die, but his daughter? Did she deserve the fate I'd set out for her? But what choice did I have? Marcos already had a buyer—he was in the process of arranging the deal. I couldn't back out. It just wasn't done.

He might not kill me if I set the girl free, but he'd make sure she wasn't free for long. And while he wouldn't kill her, he'd make her wish she was dead. The only thing I could do was make sure she was trained. Make sure she was equipped with what a slave would need to survive her new master. And then perhaps, when her buyer tired of her, I could buy her back, though freedom might mean very little to her by then.

Fuck!

Against my better judgment, I turned my attention back to the journal and flipped through the pages. The entries were sporadic, usually several months between them. She talked about me less and less until about halfway through when I stopped seeing my name altogether. But halfway—for years after she'd been taken, she'd thought about me. Damn.

The last few entries were late in her high school years. What she wrote about most was a dream she'd been having recurrently, one that obviously made her uncomfortable, though she provided no details until the second to last entry. And then I understood why it had bothered her. Taken, punished, forced to submit, to perform, over and over again. She couldn't understand why the dream kept coming. And worse, she couldn't understand why she responded the way she did, why she couldn't get it out of her mind or why it set her body on fire.

Fuck me.

No wonder she'd been unable to stop her body from responding to the things I'd done to her—they were what she'd fantasized about for years!

Reluctantly, but unable to stop myself, I turned to the last entry, and it was the same, elaborating on the same fantasy that played in her mind night after night, but there was one more thing. One little detail that had me rock hard in three seconds flat.

"I never know who it is," the entry read, "but the eyes; they're always the same, and there's something so familiar about them, comforting. Unique. Vivid blue. Vivid blue. Blue...blue... blue," she wrote over and over again down the length of the page as if she'd been racking her brain for an answer, for the owner of those eyes.

It was cocky to presume, but it wasn't. I hadn't

really paid attention to how much time she'd spent looking at me—at my eyes, specifically—but it fits now. Some part of her recognized me, and she'd been trying desperately to figure out how.

But that also meant she'd been having naughty fantasies about me? For years? What the hell?

I slammed the journal closed and tossed it in the box at my feet. This was insane. But part of me didn't think so. A large, throbbing part of me wanted to barge into her room and give her exactly what she'd been fantasizing about because from the moment I'd spied her on the street, she'd been the only fantasy occupying my thoughts.

I couldn't do it though. I wouldn't. I wouldn't let her mess with my head like this. Instead, I focused on the other content of the boxes—books. Lots of books.

I took a couple of them, figuring I'd hold onto them to give her back as rewards. Usually, I wouldn't allow outside media unless it helped to advance a slave's training—like BDSM erotica. But I found myself wanting to do something, to make amends for the plan I'd set in action.

Yeah—a book was just the thing to make up for taking away a girl's freedom and turning her into a slave.

Nothing was going to make up for it. She would come to obey me, and she'd already demonstrated that her body responded to me, but deep down, she'd hate me. Always.

And that was the reality check I'd needed. I wasn't the Derek of her fantasies, however dark they might be. A long time and a lot of shit had happened since I'd been that Derek. And there was one man ultimately responsible for all of it —her father. And he had to pay.

I wasn't certain I could feel remorse anymore, but something akin to it hit me. I didn't want to use her like this, but I didn't have a choice. The plan had been laid, and I would do what was expected of me. I would turn the most enticing woman I've ever known into the most appealing slave a master could desire.

⁓

I LEFT her alone until the next morning. It was a small favor and a punishment at the same time

—though I didn't know precisely what I was punishing her for. Making me care? Was that even possible? Or was I just off my game with my revenge so close and thrown off by the discoveries in her journal?

Still, the few hours to herself wasn't likely to set her training back any given that she was still cloistered in the room by herself, but it would give her mind and body a rest. A break before I did my damnedest to break her.

And I would succeed. I always did.

Leaving her alone though wasn't entirely a gift. It always seemed to me that leaving her alone was in a way a worse punishment to her than a spanking. The way the tension seemed to leave her body when I walked in when it should have been skyrocketing higher; how she leaned into my hand when I caressed her cheek—all signs that the solitude was like torture to her.

Morning now, I opened the door and stepped inside. The sigh of relief she didn't know I saw when I walked into the room did strange things to me. It made me imagine for just a moment she was glad to see me, and not that she was just glad to not be left alone in her cage. Maybe she worried I'd forget about her and leave her there to starve? Or maybe she was so starved for human companionship that even the monster I was, was better than no one at all.

I fed her breakfast, pleased that she didn't fight me, and then it was time to start pushing her hard. She needed to be well-prepared, and after reading through that god damned journal, I wanted this over with as quickly as possible.

"Get in the shower, pet," I told her when I'd placed the lid back on the tray.

She hesitated—the first time that morning—but too quickly, she did as she was told, following on her knees behind me while I considered her abnormally cooperative behavior at the moment. It was clearly an act, but to what end? Given her uniqueness, I wasn't quick to jump to any conclusion. Of course, it was entirely possible—and most likely—that she was hoping her good behavior would result in me leaving quickly.

However, she didn't actually like being left alone, and her hot, little body certainly enjoyed my company. So, it was possible she was only trying to avoid giving me a reason to punish her.

If so, I was more than happy to find out just how far she'd go to avoid the belt or a spanking—both of which shot a jolt of arousal to my cock at the thought.

For the first time though, there was a pang of guilt there with it. And it was time to shut that useless emotion down. I couldn't set her free, even if I wanted to, which right now, with her naked and on her knees in front of me, I had no desire to do. And that meant the only option was to make sure she was ready. It was far kinder than going easy on her when that would only lead to her suffering greatly at the hand—and whip—of her new master. And if my cock happened to benefit from the training she would need, where was the harm in that?

She stopped in front of the shower and I turned on the facet. "Get in and use the soap in the corner," I instructed her then, though it was unnecessary. I could tell by the light, floral scent of her skin that she'd showered a multitude of times on her own since arriving here. Of course, she'd never had to do it in front of me, and I was looking forward to the show.

She stepped beneath the showerhead and I

watched as water cascaded down her slender curves. When she'd squeezed the soap into her hands, she rubbed them together and then started at her neck, working her way across 'safe' zones, like her shoulders and down her arms.

"Stop," I said when she moved down to her stomach, and I stepped forward and squeezed the soap into my own hand. "Turn around," I told her and her eyes flew to mine. I cocked an eyebrow and she pressed her lips together hard, but she complied.

I rubbed the soap on the back of her neck. Her whole body seemed to sigh, though she covered it quickly, stiffening her spine.

"Take pleasure when it is offered. There is nothing wrong with it," I found myself telling her. "Your body was made to feel pleasure, to respond to touch," I continued as I worked my way down between her shoulder blades.

It seemed she was making a genuine effort, breathing slowly, deeply, and unclenching her shoulders. But it also seemed, like this, it was far more difficult for her. When her body was revved up with intense arousal, it was near-impossible for her to resist it. It clouded her thinking and probably helped to quell her father's voice in her head—the son of a bitch who'd tried to warp his daughter into thinking there was something wrong with her simply for being human, for being a woman.

Even if her innate interests leaned to the dark and erotic side, there was nothing wrong with her acknowledging them. Hell, a girl with interests like hers could have most of the world's population of men wrapped around her finger in five seconds flat. What the hell could be wrong with that? And though it shouldn't make a bit of fucking difference to me, I wanted her to believe what I was saying, to accept that there was nothing wrong or dirty about what she liked. She wasn't a whore—no matter what her fucked up father thought.

"Stop listening to it, to the voice in your head that told you there was something wrong with you. There's nothing wrong with what you like, Pet. It pleases me very much to know your body can respond to me, no matter what I'm doing to you."

To emphasize my point, I slipped my hands

around in front of her and cupped her breasts, catching her nipples between my fingers and squeezing harder than I usually would, but knowing now that her body would turn that pain into something more, something irresistible for her.

Her hands shot out to the wall to support herself as she squealed in response, but she didn't try to get away.

"Very good, Pet. Now, keep going. Wash the rest of your body."

I'd intended to just watch, but I kept my hands on her breasts as she returned to her stomach, and then her hips. I slipped down to massage her ass when her hands started soaping down one leg and then the other.

As she worked her way back up her thigh, she slowed. There was only one place left that required her attention. Her breath was already coming faster, but when I released her ass and turned her around to watch her, there were tears on her cheeks.

No, damn it. I would not feel guilty. She was still the same girl she was before I'd read that fucking journal. And my guilt did her absolutely no good. The objective trainer I'd been for years is what she needed.

"Now," I commanded.

She knew what I meant, and she slipped a trembling hand between her thighs. Her fingers glided between her folds and her breathing sped up even more.

"Very good," I said but persisted. "Tell me what you're thinking."

Her body was obviously responding—but to what? Just the feel of her slippery fingers? Or was there more to it?

She shook her head vigorously, and I reached around to spank one, firm cheek. She squealed, but her hand pressed harder against her pussy.

"I'm...I'm thinking about being watched," she spoke quietly to the shower floor as tears dripped off her chin. "...about you watching me."

Fuck. She was just too damn much.

I brushed her hand away and replaced her fingers with my own, honing in on her clit peeking out above her lips. Her body jolted and she reached out her hands to steady herself but jerked them away fast. Because it was my shoulders she'd latched onto for support.

Oh hell, yes. This was happening, I decided as I stepped into the shower with her, still fully clothed. She gasped and took a step back, but I kept my fingers on her clit...and she didn't look disappointed.

I kept rubbing her, watching her inhibitions slowly give way to the woman she kept locked inside. Little by little, her eyes glazed over and her hands returned to where they'd been, clutching my shoulders to keep herself up.

Her head tilted up then, and that surprised me, especially when her eyes met mine. She was confused, but on fire, and while I didn't particularly want to stop to punish her if she lashed out, I wanted to taste her mouth. So, I did. I pulled her close slowly until my hand between us on her clit was all that separated our bodies. The fire in her eyes blazed brighter, but the confusion grew with it.

"Stop thinking. It's not a request, Pet. Stop, or I will tie you up and whip you until you bleed," I told her sternly. Her body would make this easy for her; life as a slave would be easier for her...if she'd just stop interfering.

"I can't. I don't know how..."

"You're not a whore," I said, coming down to the heart of what plagued her. "You're a woman. A sexy as hell, submissive woman. Let it go," I demanded harshly, more feeling behind my words than I would have liked.

I swooped in and claimed her lips, feeling a possessiveness I hadn't experienced before. I knew the swift movement would throw her off-balance, making her mind reel with sensation and giving her body the chance to take over.

It wasn't instantaneous, but with my finger keeping up my pace on her clit, I won out.

Her lips parted for me and I thrust my tongue inside, a mimic of how I desperately wanted to be fucking her pussy. She moaned into my mouth as her hands slid up the back of my neck. But I had no intentions of letting her stop there.

"Take off my shirt," I said when I'd released her lips. Her fingers stilled. It was one thing for her to be passive and even to cling for support. What I was demanding now was a whole new level of difficulty. Too bad. She needed to learn. So, when she hesitated, I spanked her hard—hard enough to feel the sting in my own hand.

She yelped and jerked, thrusting her clit hard against my fingers. And when she moved to comply, her fingers were trembling so much that the buttons on my shirt were difficult for her. But eventually she managed and she slid the shirt off to where my hand against her prevented it from dropping to the ground. She raised her hands, but she didn't quite touch me. Her fingers hovered less than an inch from my chest. But she wanted to touch me. It was clear in her eyes.

So, I denied her.

"Take off my pants," I said instead and I increased my pace on her clit, just to make it a little easier on her.

She fumbled with the button and fly, eventually succeeding in her task. Her fingers lingered when she hooked them into the waist of my pants to slide them off, but whether in hesitation or as an excuse to touch me was up for debate.

Making her think she'd been given a reprieve, I stilled her hands and yanked them off myself. Her eyes went so wide that I stood still for a moment and let her look her fill. And she did look, though her cheeks flamed an even deeper shade of pink than her normal blush.

Instead of returning to her clit then, I placed my hands on her shoulders and pushed her down. My whole body was taut with anticipation.

Tears were still trickling from her eyes, but she didn't fight me. When she was on her knees, she looked up at me—an intensely erotic sight—but nevertheless, an error I would have to correct.

"Never look at your master unless you've been told to. As a slave, you are to keep your eyes down—always."

Her eyes flashed with angry fire at the reminder of her position, but still, she didn't try to get away, even with my cock less than an inch from her hot, little mouth.

"Open," I said, but I got impatient waiting for her to obey and I thrust forward and I grabbed hold of the back of her head to hold her still while I pressed against her lips. She parted for me and the head of my cock thrust in. She actually leaned up higher to accommodate me better and started working my cock deeper into her mouth.

Fuck, she was incredible. So easily aroused, and her dark, horny mind let her breech even the most stringent boundaries. By all rights, she shouldn't be working me into the back of her throat. I shouldn't be feeling the quick convulsion of her throat around the tip of my cock unless I'd forced it in there against her will.

She worked her way back to where she'd started and then took me in again. Watching her was fucking amazing—the sexy, little seductress on her knees.

She kept it up at a tortuously slow pace. If I didn't know better, I'd swear she knew exactly how to drive a man mad. After a while, I grabbed the back of her head and held her still as I started to increase the pace, thrusting deep, faster. Her hot mouth felt so fucking good. And she looked so god damned hot.

Her eyes darted up and then back down, more than once, and I should have corrected her, but I loved those eyes. I'd always loved those eyes. And they were sexy as hell now.

It was hard not to find a woman hot when my cock was filling her mouth, but this...her...I didn't think a hotter woman could possibly exist.

And she did a damn good job keeping up, taking a breath every time I withdrew so she was ready for me when I drove into the back of her throat. She was a natural. Whether she liked it or not, she was made for sex, for submission... for me. So fucking hot.

I fucked her mouth harder, faster. Every thrust made her breasts bounce enticingly. She looked up at me with her sexy as hell green eyes, and they were clouded with her own desire. Sucking my cock had kept her aroused—it was clear in her gaze.

And it was just too fucking much. My balls drew up tight seconds before I thrust in deep one last time. Shockwaves of lightning shot through my body and I spurted my cum at the back of her throat, watching her throat swallow over and over again.

I withdrew from her mouth when she'd swallowed everything I had, and I stood there watching her for a moment, just enjoying the view.

She looked up once more, but I wasn't caught up in fucking her mouth now, so I cocked an eyebrow and she dropped her gaze. But not before I'd seen what was in it. Arousal, hell yes. But it was something else that caught my attention. Or more precisely, there was a lack of something else. It was if she'd been stunned—by the way she'd responded so enthusiastically to sucking my cock? Maybe, but something wasn't right.

She was too still, like the calm before the storm. I really hoped she wasn't preparing to lash out now. I'd actually regret having to punish her after such a stellar performance. No doubt, she had conflicting feelings about what she'd just done, but as a slave, she needed to learn to subdue them, to keep them to herself. Her new master would tolerate nothing less.

I stood there for another moment, letting the showerhead massage the backs of my shoulders. Because with each passing second, the feeling grew stronger. There was a storm brewing, and it was only a matter of time before my little tempest let loose her fury.

6

SCARLETT

I knelt there on the shower floor with so many emotions coursing through me that I didn't know what to feel. Or whether to feel at all. I'd liked it. God damn it, I'd liked the feel of him in my mouth. And the sounds he'd made...knowing I was the one responsible for them...it had made me heady.

But now, I was hovering on the brink of insanity, and it was so tempting to let myself tumble over, to let it swallow me up. Whatever else it did to me, I didn't care so long as it took my mind with it. This was too much—too much even to process how I should feel.

It wasn't what the devil had done, or even how

my traitorous body had responded to it. I would gladly go back to that now, to the depraved way my body had responded to him watching me, to him touching me. I'd happily relive him forcing me to my knees and shoving his cock in my mouth and the wicked thrill that had shot through me.

Yes, I wanted those things back. I didn't want to remember what had happened after when he'd looked down at me with his vivid, blue eyes and they fell into place in my mind. I knew now why they'd seemed like a comfort when I'd first seen him, why he so easily fit into my depraved dreams.

The devil who had handcrafted my own personal hell wasn't a nameless, faceless devil at all.

He was the place I had once run to in my mind, always, the last person who'd genuinely seemed to care about me. And now, he was pure evil. He was humiliation, and pain, and hopelessness.

He was Derek...though I wished with every fiber of my being that he was anyone else.

He was talking to me. I could hear his voice

through a haze, but I couldn't make out the words. I didn't want to make them out. I didn't want to understand what he was saying.

His voice grew louder, but still no words, and I closed my eyes, trying to block it all out. For the first time, I longed for the nothingness, but I knew it wouldn't come. The devil wouldn't let it.

I felt a hand on my shoulder. Its grip was firm, but not unbreakable. He wasn't trying to haul me up. I had no idea what he was doing. I didn't want to know.

And then his hand began to shake me, and it jarred me out of whatever stunned state had gripped my mind. But all at once, everything collided.

I didn't curl up on the floor in abject misery. I didn't cry. I didn't sob. I didn't even lash out.

A scream rose up from deep inside me. I had no idea where it came from. Some conglomeration of every bit of anger, fear, bitterness, and betrayal, it knit together and rocketed outward, and I covered my own ears in some feeble attempt to block out my own sound.

He yanked me off the ground and dragged me out into the other room.

"Don't you touch me you son of a bitch. I hate you. I hate you," I screamed over and over again.

He handcuffed me to the post, but I didn't care. Finally, I opened my eyes and looked at him. It was so obvious now. How could I have missed it?

He was confused, but he was angry too. I kept screaming. I couldn't stop. I watched him stride back into the bathroom, no doubt in search of the belt on his soaking wet pants. I didn't care. His belt could never hurt me as much as I was hurting now.

I was still screaming when he came back into the room, but he wasn't holding his belt. He had a plastic cup in his hand.

Acid—it was the first thought that came to my mind, but even in my crazed state, I dismissed it. He wouldn't do that to me—though how the hell I could be so sure of that when he would do all the other things he'd done to me, I didn't know. Again, I didn't care.

The noise continued, my own ear-piercing scream that hadn't lost an ounce of momentum since it had risen up and burst forth from my lips.

He stopped in front of me, his brilliant, blue eyes full of concern. Concern?—Ha! Like a monster was capable of that emotion.

He stood there, looking indecisive for a brief moment. I didn't care. It just didn't matter to me what he did to me. If he killed me, it would be better. To put an end to this misery—yes, it sounded like a reasonable plan to me.

But he didn't raise a hand to me. Not exactly. He lifted the cup and splashed its contents on my face. No burn. It wasn't acid. Icy cold water. It was just water. But it stunned me into silence.

The scream I thought would never end died abruptly on my lips and fizzled out in my throat. "I hate you," I whispered, finding it suddenly too painful to force anything louder past my throat.

"What am I supposed to do with you, Pet?" he asked. It almost sounded like a genuine question. Almost. But I knew he didn't give a damn what I thought.

"I don't care what you do with me..." I answered anyways. "...Derek." I could barely choke out his name. It was as if by forcing it out, speaking it out loud, it made it impossible to take it back, to pretend it wasn't true.

Surprise flashed through his blue eyes—eyes I wished desperately I could claw out at that moment, to erase the proof of who he was.

"No matter whether it pleases you or not, I am master to you. Do. Not. Ever. Forget. It."

"Fuck you. I wish it had been anyone but you. Anyone!" I croaked.

"Is that so?" he seethed as anger flashed in his eyes. A possessive anger, it seemed, though it was probably just my imagination.

Then again, it wouldn't be terribly surprising. I was a thing to him. A possession to use and to break.

"Do you realize if I had been anyone else—like you so much wish—and you had dared use my name, you would have been whipped until your back was an irreparable, bloody mess. So, maybe you should think twice before wishing for a new master, Pet. But don't worry, you'll have one soon enough."

His hands were clenched into fists so tight his knuckles had turned white. I waited for the blow, to feel him letting loose his anger on me like a human punching bag. But he just stood there, silent. Ominous. Maybe he was trying to figure out how much he could hurt me without killing me so he could keep it up until he'd vented every ounce of the anger that brewed and churned inside him.

But then he turned and strode right out of the room, leaving me shackled to the post but unharmed. Why? And then his words hit me, "But don't worry, you'll have one soon enough," he'd said. A new master? He was getting rid of me. He didn't want me anymore—the result of my crazed rant?

I should be relieved, but I wasn't. Relief was nowhere in the mix of emotions that coursed through me. Bitter anger over what he'd done. Betrayal over who he was. And heartbreaking sadness that he didn't want me. He was done with me. He was going to hand me over to someone else, and in no time at all, he was going to forget about me.

His face, and all the sides of it—my childhood hero, my captor—would haunt me for the rest of my life while mine faded in his mind until I was nothing more than a fuzzy memory of the pathetic girl he'd humiliated and hurt...and discarded.

Why did that even matter to me? After all, I'd been through—after all he'd done to me—why was that what stayed at the forefront of my mind?

I hated him, even more than before when he hadn't been the boy I'd looked up to and adored. Why wasn't I glad that he no longer wanted me?

Because he was still Derek, damn it.

Whatever else he was, whatever he'd become, he was still the face of every fantasy I'd ever had. And he was still in there, somewhere, wasn't he? There had been something so tender about him all the times he'd caressed my face and ran his fingers through my hair. So many times, I'd actually let myself think he cared about me, that there must have been something that made him this way and it was the only way he could experience affection. I'd wondered what it was that had happened to him, what horrors he'd been exposed to, or suffered himself, to need this.

And then an image of the boy he'd been flashed through my mind—the handsome kid who had no idea what went on in his house when everyone else had gone to bed. He was an ordinary—albeit kind— the kid who'd tolerated me following him around like a lost puppy. My father had come to get me one night, and I'd never seen him again, not in person anyway. I ran to him in my mind often in my solitary life with my father. I remembered thinking a multitude of times that I wanted to go back there, that I'd gladly endure the bad things his father did to me if it meant I could have Derek back too.

But he wasn't that boy anymore. Something had done this to him, had turned him into the devil who needed to hurt and humiliate. As pathetic as it was, a fresh batch of tears welled up and I cried. Not for me—there would be time enough for that—but for him, for the boy, I'd loved in my little girl way, and whatever atrocities he'd suffered to turn him into something else.

He returned to the room faster than I'd thought he would. Too soon. I was still too caught up, still too confused about how I should be feeling. I couldn't handle this now. Not yet—not that what I could or could not handle mattered.

He was dressed now, his hair nearly dry, but my mind called up an image of him from not long before, naked, his cock in my mouth, his face contorted with pleasure, so much that it almost looked like pain. I hated the thrill that shot through my body, and I hated, even more, the urge to be there now, on my knees, taking in as much of him as I could, feeling the tension mounting in his body and seeing it in the expression on his face.

What the hell was wrong with me? How could I even be thinking that never mind responding to it, feeling my body revving up in anticipation—I was just as sick as he was.

He walked toward me without a word and I watched him, trying to read his expression, to figure out what he was going to do next. But when he stood in front of me, I looked away, down at the floor. Because I couldn't look any longer? Or because he'd told me that was what was expected of me? Was I actually trying to behave? Submit to him like a good, little slave? Why the hell was I doing that?

Because I didn't want him to get rid of me—the answer came to me out of the blue, stealing my breath with the shock of it. Before I had time to contemplate this new and completely insane discovery though, he reached up and unshackled me.

I dropped to my knees, not really because I was supposed to, but because it was the only way I'd be allowed to put distance between us. And I needed distance, now more than ever.

He chuckled as if he found my obedience humorous after my recent tirade. But he still reached down and stroked my cheek.

No part of me wanted to pull away. The sensations, the comfort—as much as I needed distance, I needed this too, after he'd ripped the only stability I'd ever known out from under my feet. I didn't want him to move, or talk—I just wanted to feel his hand on my face. Nothing else.

But he withdrew after a moment. "You are a slave. I don't owe you an explanation," he said, his voice harsh, which contrasted sharply with how gentle his hand had been. "I had no choice. I still don't," he said, offering what sounded an awful lot like an explanation after telling me he didn't owe me one. "Your father needs to pay for what he did. He will pay," he said succinctly as if that somehow explained everything.

My father? What the hell did my father have to do with anything? Pay?—for what? And how the hell did that have anything to do with what Derek had done to me?

"I-I don't understand," I whispered, still finding my throat too sore to do much more.

He scoffed. "You don't know that your father murdered my parents in cold blood?"

My eyes shot up to his. This had to be some sort of sick joke.

"You didn't know?" he said, not quite disbelievingly. "You don't remember the gunshots the night he took you?"

No. No, I really didn't. I'd woken up to a man's arms around me, yanking me out of bed. And I remembered what he'd said, "I promised your mother I'd take care of you, so here I am. And now, he won't have any chance to get his hands on you," he'd sneered, though I'd had no idea what he'd meant. I'd kicked and fought, but it had made no difference. And then we were in a car, driving away.

I shook my head. "What happened...Master?" I croaked, wanting to think it impossible of the man who'd taken me, but knowing it wasn't.

I could feel his eyes on me for a long time, so long I'd given up on him answering me, but then he retrieved the chair, pulled it in front of me and sat down.

"Your father would never have been allowed to leave with you," he said as he brushed his finger across my cheek. "He was a criminal. No court would have granted him custody. So, he took you and eliminated the obstacles in his way."

My heart ached, imagining the boy he'd been, suddenly orphaned. Alone. But as horrible as that was, it didn't explain what Derek had become. "What happened then," I whispered, rubbing my cheek against his hand, hoping my complacency would keep him here and keep him talking.

He shrugged. "All the kids there—including me—were sent to new foster homes." He spoke so easily it was clear he was covering something.

My fingers were trembling as I lifted them to cover his on my cheek. He could just as easily punish me for the move as accept it. But I wanted to know. I needed to understand. "And then what?" I asked when he didn't bat my hand away.

"You are suddenly full of questions, aren't you, Pet?" he said, obviously trying to brush it off.

"Yes, Master," I said, hoping to keep this side of him here.

"My foster parents were...less than ideal parents," he replied.

That's what had happened. I remembered the scars I'd seen on his back. I'd been in the midst of my screaming fit and had thought nothing of it. They did nothing to mar the physical beauty of his body, but thinking about them now... there must have been hundreds of them—thin scars, long-healed, that crisscrossed the entire expanse of his back.

I thought of the boy he'd been, and what violence must have been done to him to leave so many scars...

I choked back a sob. It didn't excuse what he'd become, but it did help to explain it. He'd become cold, unfeeling—at least, most of the time—but what other choice had there been for him? I knew from my own brief experience with him how much a person could be affected by circumstance.

I still hated him for what he'd done to me, but I also didn't. It was the most conflicted I'd ever felt. But I couldn't deny how natural it felt when I moved closer to his thighs and I stretched up higher. On my knees, I couldn't quite reach, so I wrapped my arms around his neck and drew him down to my mouth.

And then I kissed him. My lips touched his, and I waited for him to pull away, to chastise me for my behavior.

He didn't.

He let me kiss him, and when I glided my

tongue across the seam of his lips, he parted for me, letting me in while he took possession of my mouth at the same time. It was like a first kiss—the kind that dreams and fantasies were made of—and I closed my mind to everything but the man in front of me.

But he pulled away and pressed down on my shoulders, pushing me back down. "I don't know what you're trying to do, Pet, but it won't change anything. It's out of my control now."

I froze. What did he mean? What was out of his control?

"You've been sold. The transaction will take place soon. Your father will be there to see it happen. And then I will kill him."

And then I understood why he'd taken me, why he'd humiliated and hurt me. I was his revenge.

I almost laughed out loud, thinking how poorly he'd plotted his vengeance. I should let him go through with it and watch in satisfaction as his plan failed before his eyes—what disappointment he'd feel when my father barely flinched.

But then I'd belong to someone else, some new, cruel master who thought I was nothing more than a piece of meat. And Derek would be gone—that part should have bothered me the least, but it seemed to be squeezing my heart like a vice.

"It won't work," I blurted out. Self-preservation, yes—of course, I wanted to convince him not to hand me over to a new master. But something else, too. I could only imagine how much he longed for the moment when he destroyed my father, and though I should want it with every fiber of my being, I didn't want to see the hurt in him when his plan failed. I really was insane.

"There's no point in you trying to talk me out of it, Pet. It can't be undone," he said, though it sounded an awful lot like regret in the undertone of his voice.

"And it won't work," I said with certainty, though with my croaky voice, it probably sounded less than convincing.

He sighed as if dismissing the topic and went back to caressing my face.

"Your plan won't hurt my father, Derek," I said, and then immediately realized my mistake. "I'm sorry," I cried, waiting for his anger, but he let it out in a long breath and seemed to allow it to pass.

"And why not?" he said indulgently, no doubt expecting some lame excuse that he could see right through.

"He's...he's, not my father," I said, and that seemed to shock him.

He eyed me as if he could assess the truth of what I'd just said in my eyes.

"He's cared for you for a long time. It will affect him the same," he said dismissively.

It was my turn to scoff, though I reined it in quickly. "I was an obligation, and nothing more. He'd promised my mother he would look after me, and so, when he'd learned she had died, he came for me. And he has spent every day since making sure I knew what a burden I was. I don't even know why he did it—why he didn't just leave me there..." It was a question I'd asked myself and my father more times than I could count, but there was never an answer. He seemed to hate my mother, so what obligation he had to her daughter was beyond my comprehension.

"God damn it, Scar," he cursed and shot to his feet.

I scurried back, but only half-expecting his anger, and I wasn't surprised when he didn't lash out. It was the first time he'd used my name—the nickname that only he had ever used. Was I getting through to him?

But then he stormed out of the room, leaving me with no clear answer. And he left me there alone for hours. I paced my prison, my head too full to think clearly. He'd said it can't be undone...but why? Because he didn't want to undo it? He was happy to be getting rid of me, whether it served his vengeful purpose or not? If that was true, then there was absolutely nothing I could do. He would pass me onto someone else, and I'd be just as trapped, subjected to god only knew what new evils.

But maybe there was another option. Not so long ago, I would have said anyone who chose it was weak, but I wasn't weak. At least, I wasn't being weak now. I could plainly see the future that awaited me, and I was simply choosing not to accept it. I would not spend the rest of my life as some evil man's lapdog.

It was different when I thought about Derek, about forever remaining his slave, his possession. I didn't want to be just a possession to him, but I could accept it if there was no other choice. I would not die to escape it.

I shouldn't feel that way. I shouldn't so easily be able to differentiate between a life as his slave and a life as someone else's. I should hate him just as much as I'd hate any other man who did what he'd done to me. But I didn't, at least it wasn't the only thing I felt for him. It was too complicated to put into words all that I felt, but it was suffice to say I would rather live as his slave, hoping it would one day grow to something more, than not live at all. But another man...no. No, I didn't want that.

The scrape of the lock jarred me out of the dark place my mind had wandered. I dropped back down to my knees, noticing it wasn't as difficult to do as it had once been. When had that happened?

The door opened, but it wasn't Derek who walked in. The man wasn't the least bit familiar. Older than Derek, dark eyes. Dark, sinister eyes that sent a chill down my spine. I thought of what Derek had said about handing me over to a new master—was this him? Had I already lost the chance to end this before it began? Oh god, without him saying a word, I already knew I'd rather be dead than be this man's slave.

He walked toward me, and I wrapped my hands around my body, trying to cover myself. I'd gotten used to being this way with Derek, naked, with his eyes free to peruse every part of me. As wrong as it was, I'd come to like it, to feel my body revving up when his eyes grazed over me.

But this man...I didn't want him looking at me.

He stopped in front of me, looking down disapprovingly at where my hands covered me. I skittered back on my knees, but he reached out and grabbed a fistful of my hair before I could get more than a few inches. He yanked me back and my hands flew out automatically to stop from falling forward.

When I moved to re-cover myself, he yanked on my hair again, so hard I was surprised it didn't rip it out at the roots. Tears stung my eyes, but I held them there stubbornly.

"If you cover yourself again, I will break your arms to keep you from making that mistake again."

He wasn't joking. I didn't think this man was capable of it. I dropped my arms to my sides while anger and fear warred inside me. Fear won out, and I knelt there unmoving. I'd thought Derek was the devil, but I was beginning to suspect I'd been wrong.

If I'd behaved better if I'd tried to please Derek, would he still have sold me to this monster? Would he still have delighted in handing the supposed-daughter of James Donovan over to the vilest creature he could find?—certainly that's what this man was.

Or would I have mattered to him then? If I hadn't fought him constantly, would he have felt too much guilt to do something so horrible to an innocent girl? Was he even capable of that emotion, or had the years in his own hell numbed him to it? I had no answers. And why the hell was I thinking about Derek when I should have been thinking of the fastest method to check out?

"You are very appealing, slave, but you are far

from adequately trained," he said and I started to shake with fear. Pure terror, unlike anything Derek had ever evoked.

But then, maybe Derek was worse. He'd never hurt me the way I now knew this man was going to, but he'd handed me over to him. Wasn't that worse?

"Stand up. I want to inspect you, slave," he demanded.

I wanted to run, and the stupid thing about it was I wanted to run to Derek. I wanted him to wrap his arms around me and protect me, to refuse to let this monster hurt me. Tears spilled over, knowing there was nowhere to run. And even if Derek was here right now, he wouldn't save me.

I stood up, willing my knees to hold me there while the man made a tight circle around me, touching my breasts, my hips, my backside. I wanted to scream at him to get his hands off me. I was Derek's, and he wasn't allowed to touch me. But it wasn't true. And screaming at this man was sure to incite him. Derek hadn't punished me for it—when I'd screamed like a banshee and couldn't stop—but this man would.

He stopped behind me, his hands still on my cheeks, and I could feel his eyes grazing over my back.

"No wonder you're unruly. There isn't a single lash mark on you. You have not been disciplined nearly enough."

I cried harder, knowing without a doubt he was going to rectify that.

"Bend over and grab onto the backs of your calves," he said, already pressing down on my back.

Oh god, no. No, there had to be a way out. But he kept pressing and when I didn't comply, I felt a hot, vicious sting across my backside. It wasn't his hand that had struck me. No hand could hurt that much. I jerked my head back as I cried out. Bile rose in my throat—the sick monster had brought his own whip.

I started to run—it was innate. I couldn't have stopped it any more than I'd been able to stop my body's response to Derek. Derek...I begged him silently to save me, knowing he wouldn't.

The man grabbed my arm and yanked back so hard it nearly pulled my shoulder right out of its socket. I landed hard on his chest and he bent my arm back painfully, forcing me back down on my knees.

And then he leaned down until his lips were next to my ear. "You've defied me, slave, for the last time. I am going to whip you now, and I won't stop until you're unconscious. And then I'll revive you by shoving my cock up your ass, and then I'll whip you again. You will bleed, slave. And you will never defy me again."

No. Oh god, no. Please, no. Just let me die, I begged the universe. But when I opened my mouth, it wasn't death I cried for.

"Derek!"

7

DEREK

I couldn't get the image of her out of my head—first, the little girl she'd been, dragged from one hell to the next. First my sick father, then hers.

And then the young woman—the woman I'd ripped away from one hell only to thrust her into yet another. Had she ever known peace, or anything close to it? If she had, she never would again with the future I'd laid out for her.

But what the fuck was I supposed to do? The deal had been made. Marcos had finalized it two days ago. And selling a slave wasn't like selling a car. There was no changing your mind at the last minute—not unless you wanted to lose all credibility, irrevocably. And it wasn't just my reputation on the line. It was Marcos' reputation as well. I owed the man everything. My life. I couldn't do that to him. And even if I was selfish enough to do it, all for some ridiculous feeling for the girl, he wouldn't allow it. Not for her, and not even for me. I had no choice but to hand her over.

I could take her and run. The idea held appeal, but how far would we get? Marcos would hunt her down to complete the transaction. And he would hunt me down for the betrayal.

There were no options. No way out. All I could do was keep with the plan and make sure she was as well-trained as possible. That way, she'd suffer less under her new master.

Anger jolted through me at the thought of another man touching her, tasting her. It surprised me. I'd never cared about a girl enough to be the jealous type. But when I thought of her body responding to another man in the same way it had responded to me...I wanted to commit murder. I wanted to rip him apart limb from limb, and I'd take pleasure in every second of it.

Fuck!—what had I gotten myself into? She was just another girl, another slave. I'd trained a multitude of them and never once cared about another man touching them. Why now? Why this one?

Because she was different. I'd known it all along. Her uniqueness, her fight, and her fire... they had appealed to me from the beginning. I'd just never imagined those things would make me want to keep her for myself. But god damn it, that's what I wanted. What was even more fucked up was I didn't just want the obedient slave. I wanted Scarlett.

But I couldn't fucking have her.

Fuck it, I thought as something snapped inside and I strode back inside the house. Maybe I couldn't keep her. Maybe for her own good, I would have to hand her over. But she was going to be mine. Mine!

I was going to make her mine. And I knew it wouldn't be against her will. No, I didn't want her that way. I wasn't going to rape her. I was going to fuck her. I was going to tease and tempt her hot, little body until she was begging for it, and then I would make her mine.

It was a crazed plan born of anger and lust and possessiveness, one with ramifications I refused to even consider at the moment.

I stormed through the house as all the blood in my body drained to my cock. By the time I reached the door to her room, I was already throbbing painfully. I flung open the door...

...and then I froze.

It took a full second to compute what the fuck was going on. I'd been so caught up in what was about to happen that the scene in front of me seemed unreal, a figment of my crazed imagination. But it was real. Too fucking real.

Marcos' whip came down across her back and she screamed. The sound was nothing like the times I'd spanked her, even with the belt. It was filled with agony, and there were none of the signs of the lust that had wound through her body when I disciplined her. Only agony. It reached inside me and squeezed hard around my heart.

I didn't remember crossing the room, but I had, and I was grabbing the whip out of Marcos' hand.

He had her shackled to the bedpost, and the angry red lines that crisscrossed the milky white skin of her back told me he'd only just gotten started. Five, no six of them. But he was just getting warmed up because only a few of them had broken skin. If I hadn't gotten there, I could tell by the anger in his eyes that she'd done something to rile him, and he intended to teach her a lesson—a bloody lesson.

If I hadn't come back…if I hadn't foolishly decided to fuck the girl I had no business fucking…my stomach churned thinking of what he would have done to her.

I looked back and forth between them, knowing I wasn't supposed to kill him, but fighting the urge every second.

And then my stomach did more than churn. It threatened to expel everything in it. Looking back and forth between them…it couldn't be.

But it was. I don't know how the fuck I'd missed it, but it was clear as day now. Her hair, her eyes, her nose…they belonged to her mother. The shape of her face, the jut of her stubborn jaw, the tiny birthmark just below her ear...they came from her father....the man standing behind her...Marcos.

"Get out," I seethed, knowing instantly he was not unaware of the similarities between them. He knew. He knew she was his daughter, and he'd planned on whipping her, and god only knew what else.

"How dare you," Marcos seethed back as I unshackled her wrists and pulled her against me.

It was wrong the way she clung to me. I'd hurt her, too. She should be trying to flee both the monsters in the room, but she wasn't. She was holding onto me for dear life as if she knew I'd protect her.

I would, at least right now. I couldn't undo what I'd done to her, but I could keep Marcos' hands —and his whip—off her.

His own daughter. His own fucking daughter. He'd had me train her as a slave. He was going to sell her. What the fuck was wrong with him?

"You know, don't you?" I asked him, already knowing the answer.

He smiled, unperturbed. "Of course I know. What I don't know is when you started to care so much about a product? She is a means to an end, Derek, and nothing more."

"Whose end? If you know she's your daughter, not Donovan's—and I presume you've known all along—whose vengeance were you after?"

"What difference does it make to you? Donovan will die—that's all that matters to you, isn't it?"

"And how do you benefit, Marcos?" I asked though I was beginning to figure it out on my own.

"She's the product of a whore, a woman who not only fucked behind her husband's back but dared to run off on me. Every bit of her—including her child—must be destroyed. I knew when I found you that one day you would be useful to me, that your own bitter pursuit would aid me in one way or another. And you have not disappointed me, Derek. Not until now, at least."

All this time, it had never been for me. He'd said when he had found me, he'd seen strength in me, a strength that he admired, and for that he'd chosen to rescue me and give me a better life, to raise me as a son. But I had been nothing more than a tool, something he could groom and then use for whatever best served his purpose.

"Now, I was not finished with her, Derek. Give her back, and if you are still so inclined, you may have her when I'm done. But you have been lax with her, and if I have to punish her for your shortcomings, then so be it."

He reached out to grab Scarlett, and I let out a growl that didn't sound human even to me. He eyed me warily, but seemed to retreat, dropping his hand to his side. But still reeling in shock, I must have been off my game because I didn't respond fast enough when he raised the whip and started to bring it down, aiming at Scarlett's exposed flesh.

I spun around just in time to take the blow. It should have stung, but I didn't feel it. When he'd raised the whip to hit her, suddenly I was angrier than I'd ever been in my life—and I'd spent a lot of time angry.

I pushed her down on the bed and spun around to face him. "You will let her go, Marcos. I don't give a fuck what you had planned, you will find a way to undo it." He wasn't going to. I knew it before the words were out, but I had to give him the chance. Whatever his reasons, he'd rescued me from hell. He might have helped turn me into a bigger monster than the ones I'd known, but I'd let him. I owed him this, even if I knew there was no way in hell he was going to take it.

"You're upset, I understand that, Derek. And I will forgive you for it. But you will give me back my merchandise. Like you, I've waited a long time for my revenge."

Listening to him now, I realized how foolish I had been. I'd agreed to this plan, thinking that it would appease my soul, that it would somehow make up for what had been done to me. Both of us thinking we could use this girl, destroy her, to make up for wrongs that she never committed. We both deserved to die for what we'd done.

Unfortunately, today, only one of us would pay that debt.

"Let her go, Marcos," I warned him one last time.

He raised the whip again, and I knew in that split second, no matter what I said or what I did, he would never relent. If I left with her now, he would hunt us down. He'd never stop, not until I was dead and she was in hell. I deserved it...Scarlett didn't.

I lunged at him and reached up at the same time. I had his head between my hands, and without a moment's hesitation, I jerked, hard and fast, and his neck snapped with a stomach-turning crack. Such a small sound for what it signified.

I released him, the man who had been a friend, almost a father, for more than a decade, and he fell to the ground. His lifeless eyes stared up at me and my breath lodged in my throat. He was dead.

But I'd had no choice. Or, I'd had a choice, and the decision had been clear. Protect Scarlett. It was all that had mattered at that moment, and I would not regret it.

It didn't make up for what I'd done to her—I'd never be able to do that—but I would protect her.

I turned away from him to look at her. She was still on her side on the bed, right where she'd landed. She hadn't moved an inch since I'd pushed her down there, and her face seemed frozen in an expression that worried me—terror, pain, stunned disbelief.

Even when I approached her, she didn't move. Even her eyes remained fixed where they'd been, staring at Marcos' dead body. Her father's dead body. The conversation between him and I from just moments before replayed in my head and a tiny bit of guilt crept in. I'd killed her father right in front of her, not even minutes after she'd found out he was her father.

But in that way, I'd had no choice. If I hadn't done what I did right then, there was no telling when, or even if, the opportunity would present itself again. It didn't matter that she was his daughter. He didn't care. He would have tortured her just the same, maybe more so.

"I'm sorry, Scar," I said, the first apology I'd made my entire adult life feeling strange on my tongue.

My voice seemed to jar her into the moment and she looked up at me warily.

"Why did you do that?" she asked.

"He wouldn't have stopped," I explained, hoping she'd understand without me having to spell it out for her.

"But why? I'm just...a thing to you," she said as fresh tears cascaded down her cheeks.

It wasn't Marcos that had her so distraught, and that shouldn't have surprised me. Every father figure she'd ever known had been a monster. The connection meant nothing to her. But what she was asking wasn't any easier. I had no idea how to explain why I'd done what I did; why I'd been happy to view her as a thing no so long ago but now, she was the furthest thing from it. I had words for it because it was something I'd never experienced before.

So I did the only thing I could do—I ignored it. There was no sense in trying to explain something to her when I didn't understand it myself.

"Lay down on your stomach," I told her gently.

She looked up at me, confused, her eyes still filled with tears.

"We have to leave, and when we do, it will be a

long time before we can stop. You're going to be...the welts..." Why the hell was I suddenly having such a difficult time communicating? It irritated me. "Lay down," I said, more harshly than I'd intended, but this time she scrambled to comply.

I retrieved the cold cream from the bathroom—the one that few slaves ever got, medicated as it was to numb the pain. And I tried not to look at the angry welts on her back when I returned. Why they bothered me so much, I didn't know. I'd left marks on her skin, and handprints, and seeing them had turned me on. They still did when I thought about it. But the long, thin, bloody lashes across her back now, they made me angry. I wished I could revive Marcos just to kill him again for hurting her.

Ignoring my own hypocrisy, I sat down at the edge of the bed and rubbed the cream into her skin. She sucked in her breath and more tears tumbled down her when I started to rub, but the cream began to do its work quickly. She let out the breath she'd been holding and the tears began to subside. Her body began to relax beneath my fingers.

I lingered for a moment longer than I should have, massaging in small circles on her back. I wasn't ready to stop touching her, and besides, I needed that minute to solidify the plan that had begun to take shape the moment I'd opened the door and found Marcos whipping her.

It wasn't a good plan, at least not on the scale of anything that worked out for me, but it was the right thing to do. I couldn't let her go back to the life she'd known before I'd interfered. There was too much risk that she would be taken again. It wasn't like she had much of a life to go back to, even if I could offer her that.

Since I couldn't though, the only option was to take her someplace she'd be safe. A new identity, far away from her previous life—I could give her that. I'd have to hope neither her absence nor Marcos', was noticed until I returned. But assuming my luck held out, it wouldn't be difficult to stage their deaths, making it look like his car had been rigged to explode by an enemy while he was transporting his most recent slave. It would work, but I had to move fast. The moment their absences were noticed, the plan was fucked.

Now all I had to do was get her out of the house without raising suspicions. There was only one way to do it—and she wasn't going to like it one bit.

"I need you to do something you're not going to want to do," I told her.

She scoffed. OK, so making her do things she didn't want to do wasn't exactly new, but it was different now. I helped her to sit up as I tried to choose my words. She moved easily, meaning the cream had done its job.

"The only way to get you out of here is to take you right out the front door." So far the plan didn't sound too bad, right? "But you will have to be the perfect slave." Yeah—that was the catch. "There is no other way you would have been allowed to leave this room."

She nodded, but I could tell she didn't have the slightest clue what it meant.

"Why are you doing this?" she asked again.

I still didn't have a clear answer for her. "Because...because the other option isn't an option anymore."

Again she nodded, but it seemed to settle nothing in her mind. But it would have to wait. There wasn't time.

"All right, we have to go," I said and stood, moving to a section of the wall and pressing down on the wainscoting. A panel opened up in the wall and I reached inside. She was trying to look past me to see what was in there, but I blocked her view. It was just better if she didn't.

As I approached her though, her eyes widened—not that I could blame her. I hadn't gotten to preparing her for this part.

"There's no other way, Pet," I said, brushing across her cheek with my free hand, hoping it would somehow do something to calm her.

She didn't look calm, but she did look resigned. So, I went to work, fastening the collar I'd retrieved around her throat and fastening it to a leash.

"Stand up," I told her and she complied, though she kept her eyes on the other items I'd placed on the bed.

When she was standing in front of me, I picked them up and attached a small, metal clamp to each of her nipples. She squeaked in response, but she remained still. There was a long, thin chain that ran between the clamps, and one more that ran straight down to one final clamp. I knelt down in front of her and she gasped when I fastened it onto her clit.

Necessary or not, she looked so fucking hot. The last thing I wanted to do was walk her out through the house for every patron there to see. Mine!—a voice growled in my head, but I ignored it. She wasn't mine, and if all things went as planned, she never would be.

So, instead of doing what I wanted to be doing to her, I blocked it out. "Kneel, Pet," I instructed, and she went down on her knees, making it even more difficult to keep my thoughts in check. "You will remain on your knees. You will crawl, and keep your head down at all times."

She looked panicked, ready to bolt.

"You can do this, Scar. You have to do this."

It took her a moment, but she nodded. She mouthed the word 'OK' but no sound came out. Unfortunately, I wasn't quite done.

"No matter what you see, and no matter what happens, you must behave. Eyes down, and no emotion. No lashing out."

Now her whole body was trembling. This wasn't going to work if she couldn't rein it in. I reached down, running my fingers through her hair. It helped, but it wasn't enough. I crouched down in front of her and leaned in. "You can do this. I will protect you. I won't let anyone hurt you," I whispered before I leaned in further and covered her lips with mine.

By the time I pulled away, she wasn't trembling anymore. She was definitely calmer, and it was almost baffling to think that after all I'd done to her, she believed me. She trusted that I would protect her.

I stood back up and gathered the end of her leash in my hand. "Stay beside me or behind me. Never in front." And then I started forward, not giving her mind a chance to work her back up into a nervous frenzy.

At the door, she hesitated just before crossing the threshold, nearly back-stepping into the room, but she got herself under control this time and followed me out. I locked the door behind me, comforted to know the only other key to the room was in the room with Marcos' body.

The walk down the hall was quiet and she did well, keeping up despite the noises up ahead. But there was no show in the grand room this evening, which was a good thing. Seeing some of the things that Marcos arranged as entertainment—whippings, triple-hole assaults, and even bestiality if it appealed to the crowd—might send her over the edge.

Tonight though, there were only private groups scattered around the room. A slave on her knees, going down on her master; a pair of men going at another slave from both ends—all relatively mundane for this house.

She paused as we entered the room nevertheless, and I could see her taking in the various scenes, though she did well, remembering to keep her head down. I had to yank discreetly on her chain to get her moving, while the sick fuck I wished I'd attached the leash directly to the clamps instead of the collar. It made me jerk with arousal to think of tugging on those chains and watching her body with its unique response to pleasure and pain.

Once moving, it wasn't long before we had to stop again.

"Good evening, Derek," one of Marcos' patrons greeted me and I shook his hand, keeping my body loose, feigning an ease I didn't feel.

"Hello, Vincent. Are you enjoying yourself this evening?"

"I was until I saw this beauty," He motioned to Scarlett and then leaned into stroke her back and along the curve of her ass. One more second, and I feared I wasn't going to be able to stop myself from breaking the man's hand. Fortunately, he had the sense to remove the offending hand before I had the chance.

"She really is something. I'd like to have her for a while," he said, fully expecting me to hand her over.

It was going to seem strange when I didn't, but Vincent wasn't interested in just touching the merchandise. He had an anal fetish, and he preferred the slaves dry so he could make them bleed. And there was no fucking way I was letting him do that to her. If anyone got to fuck her tight, little ass hole, it was going to be me. And I had no interest in making her bleed. Scream—yes, in pleasure, not the kind of pain Vincent liked to subject the slaves too.

"I'm afraid Scarlett isn't available this evening, but Marcos always has an abundance of slaves who would be happy to accommodate you."

He looked displeased, irritated over being deprived of what he wanted, and his hand returned to her ass, skimming between her cheeks this time, no doubt seeking out the hole he'd been planning to use.

It was either time to leave or kill him. And I could tell by the way Scar's body had stiffened, I had seconds to go out of there or else I might as well kill him. It would draw no less attention than the scene she was about to cause.

"Tomorrow night. I'll let Marcos know you've reserved her," I said and then yanked on her chain and walked away without giving Vincent a chance to reply.

She followed eagerly, but I could feel the tension in her and the tiny sniffling noises she made that meant she was trying desperately to hold back tears. Just one more minute—assuming we didn't run into anyone else.

I actually breathed a sigh of relief when we reached the door to the yard. It was less conspicuous than going out the front door. It wasn't uncommon for some of the patrons to take the slaves out in the yard to make them defecate on the lawn. Where that got fun, I had no idea, but then again, one might say my fetishes wandered outside the realm of normal, too.

Once outside, I was pleased to find there was no one else around. I led her around the yard to the garage, used my key to get in, and then hurried her over to my car. I opened the trunk and then helped her to her feet. She looked at the open trunk warily.

"No one can see me leaving with you. Once we're past the guards, I'll let you out."

She nodded and even went climbing in, but the movement tugged on the chains between her clamps. She froze and squealed in response, making my cock jerk in my pants.

I leaned down to release the clamp on her clit and couldn't help but watch the expression on her face as blood rushed back into the sensitive nub all at once. And I also couldn't resist the urge to rub her, just for a minute, just until her hips started to writhe and a tiny moan escaped her lips.

I released her then and helped her to climb in the trunk, though I left the nipple clamps on her—because that was just the kind of twisted man I was. Besides, they looked so fucking sexy on her. What guy would have been quick to take them off?

I closed the trunk after one last look and then slid behind the wheel. I made it past the guards without a hitch and drove for a few miles just to be safe. When I pulled over on the side of the road and opened the trunk to let her out, I'd expected to find she'd taken the clamps off on her own.

She hadn't.

I swallowed hard and helped her out. I took the clamps off then, but as I released one and then the other, I sucked her nipple into my mouth, feeling the arousal coursing through her body in response to both sensations.

As tempted as I was to linger, we were nowhere near out of the woods yet. I grabbed the spare shirt I kept in the trunk and handed it to her. She clasped it awkwardly but made no move to put it on. I'd kept her naked for so long, apparently, she didn't quite believe I was telling her to cover up now. It really was a shame to cover up that body—and if we ended up getting pulled over, no doubt that body could get us out of any speeding ticket. Still, I didn't relish the idea of sharing it—even the sight of her sexy curves—with anyone.

So, I took the shirt from her and held it out, nodding for her to slip her arms into the sleeves. She remained still while I fastened the buttons. I was already anxiously awaiting the moment I could rip the shirt off her.

But then it hit me. There was no moment. If I went through with my plan—which I had every intention of doing—the glimpse I'd gotten of her before I'd buttoned up the shirt was the last glimpse I was going to get. When we got where we were going, I'd be leaving her there. Alone.

And I wasn't going to see her, or her hot body, ever again.

Damn, I really didn't care for the strange way the thought made my chest ache and my eyes sting. It was unfamiliar and unwelcome.

And I had a job to do. That's what this was now. Not the job I was used to, but a job nonetheless. I was going to make sure she was safe. It was all that mattered. Somehow, at some point, making sure no one could ever hurt her again—the way both her father and I had—it became the most important thing in the world. All I had to do was get her to where we were going and leave her there. Just walk away. It was easy.

So why the hell did it feel like the hardest thing I'd ever done?

8

SCARLETT

We drove for several hours—four hours, which I could tell because there was a clock. A real clock. The first one I'd seen since he'd taken me. But I had no idea where we were going, or how much longer it would be before we got there.

Derek had been quiet the whole time. And I hadn't tried to engage him in conversation. What was I supposed to say? So much had happened since he'd walked into my prison and found that man whipping me. That man...my father. My real father. And now he was dead. I didn't know how I was supposed to feel about that.

I didn't know how I was supposed to feel about anything—least of all the man sitting next to me, driving me further and further away from my prison. Why was he doing it? Why had he done any of it?

I wanted to blame it on his temper—that was the reason he'd taken hold of the man and snapped the life right out of him. But I'd made Derek mad countless times, and not once had it seemed like he'd responded in anger. He'd hurt me, yes, but it had always seemed like he'd done it with a completely level head. I wasn't sure that made it better, but it did tell me he didn't act on impulse, not that kind.

And so as much as I wanted to deny it, I knew he'd done it for me. He'd killed a man…for me. I didn't know how to feel about that either. People seldom did anything for me, never mind taking a person's life to keep me safe!

And then he'd helped me escape—at least, I thought that was what he was doing. It hadn't felt like much on an escape when he'd trussed me up in collar and clamps and paraded me through that wretched house. When that man had approached us, when he'd touched me where nobody but Derek ever had, it had taken everything I'd had to keep from lunging at him with teeth and claws drawn.

But Derek said he would keep me safe. He wouldn't let any of them hurt me. And he'd kept his promise. Though my skin crawled to think about that man's hands on me, he hadn't hurt me, and Derek had hurried us out of there before he could. Though I wondered if it was more for his benefit than mine. The rage that had coursed through him when the man touched me had been palpable in the air.

I should care. I was still painfully aware that this was insane. But it had sent an odd thrill through me to see him responding so possessively. I was his. Only his. That man had no business touching me because I belonged to Derek. And God help me, that was exactly what I wanted.

And it was beginning to seem like he wanted it too. Why else would he have done all that he did? Why else would he have taken me away from there when just hours before he'd been determined to sell me?

The same thrill that coursed through me earlier,

pulsed through my veins now. He wasn't going to sell me. He was going to keep me. I would be his, and maybe the emotion I'd seen in him when the man who was my father had been hurting me would grow. And then I would be more than just a possession to him. I would be a woman. His woman.

My stomach growled, not for the first time in the past hour. But I kept my mouth shut. Derek had been the one to feed me, to bring my meals regularly. He must know I was hungry. If he wasn't stopping to feed me, then there had to be a good reason for it.

So, I wasn't surprised when we pulled off the highway a short while later and he pulled up to a motel with an all-night diner out in front of it.

"Stay here," he said, and he eyed me for a moment.

"I won't leave. I promise," I said, and I meant it. I didn't want to leave. I never wanted to leave him.

And I must have been convincing because he nodded and hopped out, striding across the lot to the motel office. I watched the door once he'd gone inside, waiting for him to return.

I'd expected him to go to the diner, not the motel. Were we stopping for the night then? I suppose it made sense. He'd somehow become something more than human in my head, but he was human—flawed and beautiful—and probably tired.

I watched him walk toward me a few moments later, and like before, he struck me as some graceful predator. But this time, though my breath came quicker and my heart sped up, it wasn't fear I felt as he came closer.

He opened the door to my side. "Come on, Pet," he said as he extended his hand. I took it, thinking that no one had ever opened a car door for me before. It was strange how special such a simple gesture could make a person feel.

Once out though, I was immediately aware of my state of dress. The shirt came down to cover the tops of my thighs, but little more. It had been fine in the car, with only Derek to see me. Now though, with people coming and going, it was uncomfortable. But he kept my hand in his and pulled me along with him to a motel room ten yards from the car. It was the first time he'd let me walk beside him. It felt...human—a man and a woman, holding hands and walking toward a motel room.

That thought made my step stutter. There was a very well known reason for a couple to get a motel room in the middle of the night. Is that what we were going to do?

Tremors of fear and excitement shot through me together, but the excitement, the anticipation, quickly outdid the fear. Heat settled low in my abdomen and set my nether region on fire.

Once inside the room, he released my hand and I dropped to my knees—because that was what he'd expect from me, wasn't it?

"No, Pet. Stand up," he said, not unkindly.

Apparently, that hadn't been what he wanted, but then, I was at a complete loss as to what to do. I got up and stood there awkwardly. I wanted to touch him. I wanted him to know I wasn't going to fight him on this. That I wanted this. But before I could work up the nerve, he spoke.

"I'm going to get food. Don't leave the room."

I nodded right away and he didn't eye me this time. He turned the door handle and strode out. But what was I supposed to do? I thought ahead to what was coming...I'd shower quickly—that's what I would do.

I hopped in fast, wanting to be out long before he returned. And I scrubbed my body quickly. But when my hands scrubbed over the welts on my back, they flared to life. I sucked in my breath, but kept going, listening for the door.

I was out before he returned, so I dried in a hurry, moving gingerly over my back. It was too late though. Whether it had been my hands, or the water had washed away the cream that had been taking out the sting, I didn't know, but they hurt now and it irritated me. I didn't want to be distracted, not by the wounds that man had left on my body.

Trying my best to block it out, I returned to the main room. Since he still hadn't returned, I sank to my knees to wait for him, but I squeezed my thighs tight like I'd learned to do before to keep my heels from digging into the angry welts.

Moments passed, but I wasn't concerned. My master...Derek wouldn't leave me here.

My thighs started to ache, but when I sank down lower onto my heels, I shot right back up. The ache wasn't nearly as bad as the welts.

He returned then, but he stopped when he saw me. There was a fire in his eyes and it rekindled the fire inside me, but there was something else, too. Frustration? Disappointment? What had I done? Thinking that my awkward position was the only possibility, I sank down onto my heels, biting my lip against the gasp that tried to rush out.

He placed the bag and tray he'd brought back with him on the bed and came to stand in front of me. He brushed my cheek like I'd grown accustomed to him doing, and I nestled against his hand. Still, something wasn't right.

"Stand up, Pet. You don't have to kneel anymore."

Why not? What was going on? I stood though, breathing a brief sigh of relief when my heels were no longer digging into the welts.

"I've gotten you enough food to last you until morning," he said, "And I'm going to leave you with enough money to take the train that leaves here at eleven-o-clock tomorrow morning. When you arrive at your destination, there will be a P.O. box with documents you'll need. I'll have them sent there before you arrive. You'll have a new ID. I'm sorry, but your last name will be different. You won't be able to use 'Donovan' anymore. Once you have the documents, you'll find a bank account in your new name. There will be more than enough money to get you started."

He'd lost me at the word 'leave'. He was leaving? No. I didn't want him to leave. "What?" was all I could manage to get out as the world began to spin.

"Scar, it's OK. There will be nobody to hurt your anymore...I won't be there to hurt you," he said.

"No, please, M-Master. I'll be good. Don't go," I cried when what he'd said had begun to sink in.

"You don't really want that. I've trained you to think that's what you want, but it isn't. Soon, you'll see that," he said, brushing away a tear that trickled down my cheek.

He turned away fast, and I realized he wasn't just leaving. He was leaving now.

"No!" I cried and lunged for him before he'd even taken a step.

My naked body, pressed against his, was having an effect. I could feel it in him. So, I held on tight, pressing my body intimately against his.

"I don't want you to go. I'm not crazy. And I'm not brainwashed. I can't explain why or how it happened. And I know I should feel this way, but I do." I loosened my grip enough to move around until I was standing in front of him. "I want you, Master, in...in all the ways a woman can want a man."

"Oh fuck, Scar," he cursed, but then his lips were hard against mine and his arms were around me.

He pulled me closer, but as his hands dug into my back, I couldn't stop the cry that slipped out. He froze, and then he dropped his hands. No. No.

But instead of leaving, he pulled out the cream he'd apparently tucked into his pocket.

"Lay down, Pet," he said, and I immediately complied.

Like before, the cream stung at first, but then, as his hands continued to work it into my flesh, the pain began to fade. He kept it up, rubbing in small circles from my backside to the middle of my back, and different sensations rippled through my body. For the first time, I had no desire to resist. I sighed and a tiny moan escaped my lips when his fingers kneaded my cheeks. It felt so good like he knew the perfect combination to soothe and arouse at the same time.

His hands started to branch out further, down the backs of my thighs and up to my shoulders. Without being told to do it, I rolled over, and I boldly pulled his hands back when he went to drop them by his side. I placed them on my breasts and thrust my chest harder against his hands.

He didn't move at first, and I thought there might be no way to persuade him, but then he yanked one hand out of my grasp and caught both my wrists in his. And then he yanked my arms over my head, pinned against the mattress.

His other hand palmed my breast, kneading, and then teasing my nipple before moving onto the other. He kept me pinned there while he lowered his mouth to one nipple. I moaned as he sucked it into his mouth, and then I squealed when his teeth bit into me, that exquisite combination of pain and pleasure that drove me wild.

"You don't understand what you're asking, Pet," he said when he'd released my nipple, leaving it bereft of sensation until his fingers took over. "What I am, what I want, what I like to do to you...that hasn't changed," he said, and a blaze of heat shot through me, thinking of the things I knew he liked to do to me.

He must have seen the heat because he cringed and he let out a long breath. "Fuck, Scar, you've got to stop," he said between gritted teeth.

"I-I didn't do anything," I said, but I didn't bother resisting the urge to press my breast against his hand. It was intoxicating to see the way he was responding to me.

Something changed in him, and his resistance gave way. All of a sudden, he wasn't fighting me anymore.

But that didn't mean he was going to make it easy for me.

"Open your legs and tell me you want me to touch you," he demanded.

I parted my legs easily, but the words hovered on my lips while my cheeks flamed. "Please touch me," I said finally.

He grinned slyly. "Where, Pet? Where do you want me to touch you?"

My flesh tingled in anticipation and that seemed enough to make me bolder. "I want you to touch my pussy. I want to feel your fingers on me."

His hand slipped between my parted thighs and his fingers glided across my wet lips. I was so primed, so on fire, that the glide made my whole body jerk. He kept it up, lightly, teasing. He was trying to drive me insane!

"My clit. Please," I whispered, trying to direct him to where I needed him, but he chuckled and kept up with the light glide.

"Show me," he said.

"What do you mean?"—not that it was difficult to guess.

"You know what I mean. Put your fingers on your clit and show me how you like it."

He'd touched me expertly before, so I knew he didn't need my guidance. This was part of the things he liked to make me do. And I was aroused enough that I didn't hesitate. My cheeks burned hotter, but I slipped the hand he'd released down, covering my clit and rubbing fast, trying to quench the fire that was blazing hotter than ever.

His eyes were focused on what I was doing, and it made me even hotter to know he was watching me. I writhed against my own fingers, while my moans grew louder.

Then he put his hand over mine, slowing my fingers. "Don't rush it," he said.

I obeyed, but it was different, moving slowly, languidly on my clit while he watched. It was an entirely new kind of erotic.

And then he released my other hand and stood up. He moved to the end of the bed and leaned down until his mouth was just inches from me.

I could feel his breath on my wet lips while his eyes stayed fixed on my fingers. And then it wasn't only his breath I felt.

His tongue glided across my lips, parting them, and I felt his tongue at my opening. He pressed inside and I couldn't slow it down. I rocketed high no matter how slowly my fingers moved. His tongue penetrated me, stroking inside me, and I tumbled over the brink.

"You're so fucking responsive," he said, not displeased. And then he stood up and his fingers moved to the buttons of his shirt.

"Wait," I said and shot straight up.

He chuckled. "What is it?" he asked indulgently—as if he didn't know.

"I want to...May I please undress you?" I said, only mildly surprised by my own boldness.

He nodded and I crawled to the edge of the bed. On my knees, I unbuttoned his shirt. My hands still trembled, but not like before. I slipped the shirt off his shoulders and let it fall to the floor while I took in the sight in front of me. Broad shoulders, chiseled chest, his arms covered with sinewy muscle. My mouth watered just looking at him.

I glided over his hard flesh and he let me. And he didn't stop me when I leaned forward further to sample his skin with my lips. I'd only intended to see what it was like—to kiss a man like that—but one press of my lips against his throat, and I was addicted.

I covered every inch of his neck, and then his shoulders, and then I moved lower, kissing a trail down his chest. When my lips brushed across one nipple, he sucked in his breath. So, I tested the other nipple, and the response was the same.

A powerful tremor rippled through my body, realizing there were multiple things I could do to make him respond. But before I could test the waters any further, he yanked me upright.

"You have a very talented mouth, Pet, but unless you want me to put it to better use, I suggest you rest those lips."

I knew what he meant, and yes, I did want to do that. But I also wanted something else. And it was going to happen. He wouldn't change his mind now, would he?

Just in case, I reached for the fly of his jeans before he could stop me. And he didn't brush my hands away when I unzipped it. I gasped though when his cock sprung free—I'd almost forgotten the massive size of him.

He chuckled, though whether at my boldness or my response to the sight of him, I didn't know.

"Eager, are you?" he asked, but he didn't seem the least bit bothered by it.

"Yes." And just in case there were any misunderstandings about what it was I so eagerly wanted, "I want you," I said, my voice stronger than I would have expected.

He eyed me for a moment, again contemplating something. I hoped he wasn't debating whether to deny me. I didn't want to be denied. Not of this.

"Please," I whispered, hoping to persuade him.

He shucked his pants without taking his eyes off me, and I was fairly certain that meant I'd won.

And then, instead of telling me what to do, he climbed on the bed and took me with him, laying me back while he hovered over top of me. I reached for him again. I wanted to feel him beneath my fingers, but I'd barely made contact when he captured both my hands in one of his and yanked my arms high up over my head.

"Tell me what you want." The sly light was shining brightly in his eyes, but I also got the feeling he needed to hear me say it. He needed to know this was what I wanted.

"I want you to fuck me," I told him, blushing only a bit more than I already was.

He looked at me. He wasn't deciding anything—he'd already made this decision. He was just looking at me. He was making me wait—we both knew it. And while I was probably supposed to lie there complacently, I couldn't. I thrust my hips up toward him, imploring him. I tried to lean up enough to reach his lips, but the way he had me pinned kept him out of my limited reach.

"Please, Master. Fuck me." I felt empty even

though I had no idea what it was like to be filled. I wanted to know. Now.

And he was done tormenting me. He positioned himself between my thighs and I could feel the head of his cock at my opening. Yes, this is what I wanted. I writhed, trying to draw him in, but he held still, refusing to give in. When I stopped, he nodded, as if to tell me that's what he'd been waiting for—for me to stop trying to take charge.

And then he was inside me, stretching me. He moved slowly, filling me one overwhelming inch at a time. So stretched, it felt like I was burning around him, but the sensation began to fade, and in its place arose a sense of fullness, completeness. Thousands of nerve endings fired, making me want to move...writhe...thrust...fuck.

But he kept up the exquisitely slow plunge. And then I could feel him pressing up against the barrier inside me. He seemed to hesitate, though his body thrummed with tightly strung energy.

"Please," I begged shamelessly. I didn't care

about the stupid barrier. I wanted him inside me, filling me completely.

Reluctant acquiescence—for once, he didn't want to hurt me. At least, not like this. But he got it over with quickly. One, hard thrust and he was through.

The pain of my tearing hymen seared through me, but it fizzled quickly. He was inside me, every bit of me filled with his cock.

He remained still for a moment—I think he was giving me time to adjust to him. But when I wriggled against him, letting him know I was ready, he withdrew, only to plunge back in. Thousands upon thousands of nerve endings. Sensations. A fire that burned bright, and brighter still every time he thrust inside me.

I needed to move with him, so I wrapped my legs around his hips, drawing him in deep and thrusting my hips up to meet him. I needed to touch him, but my hands were still pinned above my head. I tried to tug them free, but he held tight.

"What is it you want, Pet?" he gritted out between clenched teeth.

"I want to touch you. I want my hands on every part of you." I was too caught up in the fast climb for embarrassment or modesty.

He released my hands and I reached out, running my fingers greedily over every inch of him I could.

His pace increased, and his sounds began to mingle with mine. Loud. Too loud, I thought vaguely, thinking of all the people passing by outside. But I didn't care. I didn't care if the whole world could hear us, or see us, just so long as Derek kept fucking me.

At some point, his pace had begun to lose its rhythm. Every thrust was frantic. Hard. Pounding into me and bringing me so close to the brink, I wasn't going to be able to fight it back much longer.

And when he looked down at me, there was a wildfire blazing in his eyes, and something else too – something that was both fierce and tender. I couldn't hold back any longer. My hips thrust up to meet him one last time and I screamed out his name as tsunami-size waves of the most exquisite pleasure surged through my body.

"Oh fuck, Scar. Your pussy feels so fucking good," he groaned then and I could feel him swelling deep inside me as pulse after pulse of his liquid heat began to fill me.

He stayed there inside me for a long time while the aftershocks of my orgasm continued to ripple through me. Eventually, he withdrew though, and I couldn't believe how empty I felt. It was as if I'd been incomplete my whole life and finally, with him inside me, I'd been whole.

He laid down next to me and pulled me against his chest. I could hear his heart beating, and I knew it was a sound I would never tire of hearing. He was silent for so long that I began to think he'd fallen asleep, but then he spoke. And I wished he hadn't.

"I have to go, Scar. And you need to be on that train tomorrow," he said, and my world started to crumble.

"Don't go." It was all I could force out, but in those two words was every reason, every bit of feeling I had, every ounce of love that I felt for him. Yes—love. I was done denying it. It was what I felt, right or wrong.

"I have to go back there. I have to get rid of the body before anyone realizes he's missing. If I don't..."

"Then I'll go with you. And I'll help. And then we can leave—together."

"No, we can't."

Suddenly I was tired of being told what I could and could not do. Maybe what we'd just done had banished the fear of him I'd still felt. Or maybe, in my post-orgasmic stupor, I wasn't thinking straight. Whatever the reason, I refused to listen to him. Not in this. He could tell me to kneel, to crawl, to hand over my body and soul, and I'd do it. But he could not tell me we couldn't be together.

The thought occurred to me that perhaps Derek didn't want us to be together. That, while he couldn't bring himself to sell me, he was otherwise happy in his life without me. But no, if I was being honest, and not letting doubt and worry reign supreme, I could clearly see that he did want me. Something had changed in him since that first day, and he wanted what I could offer more than anything he'd ever had before.

And if I was wrong, too fucking bad.

"Yes. We. Can," I said as I pushed off him and sat up. "You put me through hell, and I've come out of it stronger. I know myself better than I ever did before and I've accepted parts of myself that I never thought I could. And you, you're not the same person you were when you first walked in that room—and you know it. Maybe it's crazy—the circumstances that brought us to where we are—but we're here. I'm not going anywhere without you. And you're not leaving here without me."

It was true. It was all true. What he'd done may have been wrong, but would I have gotten to this point without him? And if what he'd put me through meant he could cast off his dark past and live as a whole person again...well, I'd do it all over again if I had to. Because that's what you did for someone you loved. For the man who had all your heart, you were willing to go to hell and back.

We'd been there, in hell, in the years we'd been apart and in the weeks or months since being thrust together—I really had no idea how much time had passed, now that I thought of it. But we'd been in hell, and now we were walking out of its flames together. Together—whether he was ready to admit he wanted it or not.

He was silent, eyeing me, assessing me. But I wasn't backing down. Not this time.

Eventually, he leaned up. He didn't say a word. He held me tight against him and he kissed me. A kiss that was filled with all the things he wasn't ready to say—maybe he didn't even know how to say. But he meant them, the emotions he conveyed with his mouth instead of his words.

And that was fine with me because we had more than enough time now—all the time in the world, actually—to learn to say all the things we wanted to say. His kiss told me he was staying, and that was all that mattered.

We would have to go back to hell together, but just for a little while. Just long enough to cover our tracks so that no demons could ever follow us out.

And that's just what we did. Twenty-four hours later, we stood in front of the blazing wreckage, the funeral pyre of a man who had been a friend, and a father—though he was worthy of neither title.

I still didn't know how to feel. Neither did Derek, I think. But we would sort it out together. Together—that was all that mattered.

We walked away without a backward glance. I held two thick envelopes tight in my arms. One contained our future—all the documents we would need for our new life. The other held the past—the documents, the list of patrons, pictures—the proof we would mail to the state's FBI branch. Marcos was dead, and soon, his empire would be too.

And our new life had only just begun.

∽

To be continued...

Preorder the next book in the Beauty and the Captor series:

Her Savior

ACKNOWLEDGMENTS

Thank you for taking the chance to read my book. I hope you have enjoyed reading this book as much as I've enjoyed writing it.

Even though Derek and Scarlett's story is only starting, I'm already feeling those characters come to life, and I have so much in store for them in the next two books!

I hope you will continue reading the series, and I truly hope you enjoyed this story. If you'd like, please leave a review for the book. Your support really means a lot and keeps me going.

I wrote this book for the readers who crave

darkness. Keep reading. The story has only just begun…

Nicole

MORE INFORMATION

The Beauty and the Captor series:

Her Beast

Her Savior

Her Dom

If you enjoyed this book, please consider leaving a review on Amazon! I would really appreciate it!

Made in the USA
Monee, IL
04 February 2021